The
Miller/Romero
Connection

The
Miller/Romero
Connection

Was Mad Max the survivor of the Zombie Holocaust?

Written by:

Peter D Fleming

Order this book online at www.trafford.com
or email orders@trafford.com

Most Trafford titles are also available at major online book retailers.

Printed in the United States of America.

ISBN: 978-1-4269-7244-7 (sc)
ISBN: 978-1-4269-7245-4 (hc)
ISBN: 978-1-4269-7246-1 (e)

Library of Congress Control Number: 2011909720

Trafford rev. 06/14/2011

 www.trafford.com

North America & International
toll-free: 1 888 232 4444 (USA & Canada)
phone: 250 383 6864 ♦ fax: 812 355 4082

Preface

One might wonder how the conclusion might be drawn showing a relationship between two such differing storylines. One may even further wonder how I could be so attached to such artistic works, which clearly seem to show a vastly different world. But are the worlds depicted in these works really so different? They share many of the same elements do they not? The need for survival after a holocaustic event, recreation of social order out of chaos, and grim reality that humans are in fact the true threat to humanity...

You might still be thinking that this still doesn't explain how one could come to combine these stories into one reality.

Well the first point is rather easy to explain. I grew up with an overly active imagination and a deep joy for the entertainment value of movies (there are those that say I am obsessed... I would say that seems a bit extreme). I have always had a strong appreciation for a movie, especially one which could tell a good story, or create a reality out of the unreal. One must admit that both George A Romero and George Miller are superb story tellers. They can both create realistic action sequences, with touch of suspense, while maintaining the human element.

The stories told by these masters, also present a deep understanding of how humanity acts and reacts to adversity. We, being the top of the intellectual food chain, pride ourselves with our ability to control the world around us, with all our toys and inventions of modern society. We see ourselves up high on the moral ground, kings and queens with the earth as our realm. But when something comes along and dethrones us (be it war, natural disasters, financial ruin...) we quickly forget our precious humanity.

Survival then becomes our master.

I know this to be all too true. I have witnessed it on countless occasions, while serving in the Armed Forces, in one form or another for over twenty years, as National Guard, Active Duty Military, and as a Security Contractor, in peace time and during war. I have supported various agencies during counterdrug operations, been a peace keeper, and assisted in the 'liberation' of countries. I have done all this and more in Central America, Europe, the Middle East, and various duty assignments in the continental United States.

During these various missions I have seen how ordinary people cope with the loss of civil services, loss of governmental controls, and the loss of what one would consider 'normal'. Basically, one could say, the complete loss of all hope. I have seen how the strong lord over the weak. I have witnessed people lose their humanity and turn to a more primal, if not primitive, existence just to survive. But, also I have witnessed society as it begins to rebuild, to recreate itself and grow into something else altogether.

To most, those films may seem like mere entertainment but, they are so much more than that. They are windows into the very soul of what it means to be human. If one would like to be anthropologist and/or a sociologist I think it should mandatory to study those films. Then go to one of the regions of the world that is currently in conflict and only then would everything become clear…

What these master story tellers have done was to show the true side of humanity. I have witnessed the good, almost naïve viewpoint, that many survivors cling to. There are thousands of stories to be told of how one copes and triumphs over adversity… But there are many more horror stories to tell…

I greatly appreciate and thank both George A Romero and George Miller for their artistic yet realistic approach to humanity. I wish more visionaries would follow their model. I also hope they continue to bless us with great stories of what it means to be human…

TABLE OF CONTENTS

SECTION I

-Introduction-

SECTION II

-The Films-

SECTION III

-Stories Linked-

SECTION IV

-Misc Information-

SECTION V

-The People who Died-

"The good, say the mystics of spirit, is God, a being whose only definition is that he is beyond man's power to conceive - a definition that invalidates man's consciousness and nullifies his concepts of existence. The good, say the mystics of muscle, is Society - a thing which they define as an organism that possesses no physical form, a super-being embodied in no one in particular and everyone in general accept yourself.... The purpose of man's life, say both, is to become an abject zombie who serves a purpose he does not know, for reasons he is not to question."

-Ayn Rand-

"The pornography of violence of course far exceeds, in volume and general acceptance, sexual pornography, in this Puritan land of ours. Exploiting the apocalypse, selling the holocaust, is a pornography. For the ultimate selling job on ultimate violence one must read those works of fiction issued by our government as manuals of civil defense, in which you learn that there's nothing to be afraid of if you've stockpiled lots of dried fruit."

-Ursula K. LeGuin-

"I think most military men think it's just another weapon in the arsenal... I think there are many times when it would be most efficient to use nuclear weapons. ... I don't believe the world would end if we exploded a nuclear weapon."

-Retired US Air Force Chief of Staff General Curtis E. LeMay (1968)-

"We in Australia, of course, are British, if I may say so, to the boot heels... but we stand together...our people stand together... till the crack of doom."

-Sir Robert Menzies- 12th Prime Minister of Australia

SECTION I

-Introduction-

Film Genre Basics

The Zombie/Nuclear Holocaust Genre 101

George A Romero/George Miller Intro

Film Genre Basics...

Throughout history story tellers have told tales of woe, heartache, and triumph. They told of monsters, disasters, war, personal conflict, and battling the demons of other worlds. These were first passed on by word of mouth, then written, acted out in plays, published in books, and finally played out on the big screen. Audiences are often times left wanting more, which creates the sequels and knock-offs. Though hundreds of thousands of films have been made, and continue to be produced, only a few will stand out.

There are countless genres and sub-genres that filmmakers use to categorized their projects. Most people are familiar with the basics. Whenever one goes to the old video stores, visit 'I-Tunes', or get a movie from a friend, one question we always want answered, what kind of movie is it? We want to know is it a comedy, romance, war, history, action/adventure, sci-fi, or horror film. Then we look at what it is about and who is in it.

Often times the films destined to become a classic (at the cult level at least) are made with small budgets and a cast of relative unknowns, 'Desperado' (1995) and 'The Blair Witch Project' (1999). These are the obscure flicks that didn't get much press but were marketed by word-of-mouth, blogs, and other such avenues. Sometimes these gems are left forgotten until the star becomes a famous actor.

Other times the fans themselves have a voice loud enough to be heard and the film makes a comeback, or it gets remade with a bigger budget... which is often at the cost of the film's original charm, 'The Italian Job' (1969 and 2003) and 'Alfie' (1966 and 2004). Sometimes the remake can be a great jumpstart to a whole new franchise opportunity, 'Ocean's Eleven' (1960 and 2001), followed by 'Ocean's Twelve' (2004) and 'Ocean's Thirteen' (2007).

It seems everyone loves an adventure story. The proof is in the box-office and the numerous sequels then launched, whether it is 'Indiana Jones' (1981, 1984, 1989, 2008), 'Superman' (1978, 1980, 1983, 1987, 2007), or 'Star Wars' (1977, 1980, 1983, 1999, 2002, 2005)… everyone loves a good adventure. This is further proven by the fact that each of these either came from or spawned numerous comics, spin-offs, books, cartoons, TV series, and toys/merchandise to become multi-billion dollar franchises.

With the love of a good adventure in mind, everyone also loves a good battle against some evil or sinister force. 'Friday the 13th' (1980, 1981, 1982, 1984, 1985, 1986, 1988, 1989, 1993, 2001, 2009,), 'A Nightmare on Elm Street' (1984, 1985, 1987, 1988, 1989, 1991, 1994, 2010), and 'Halloween' (1978, 1981, 1982, 1988, 1989, 1995, 1998, 2007, 2009, 2012) are just a couple examples of our fascination with the horror genre. (These are also very profitable for the production studios!) Like the adventure films, these too have spun-off numerous adaptations, TV series, merchandise and more.

Both genres draw large crowds who sit in morbid hunger lust waiting to see who the next victim will be. Many root for the victims and many for the evil doer. The same can be said for any movie but when it comes to adventure and horror, when done properly, we sit glued waiting to see what will happen next. Can the hero outsmart the adversaries, will the group survive the maniac. Then when the sequels come out we march out to see what the new story will tell. These are just a couple of genres that capture our imagination.

Since the very beginning of the film industry movies have been based off a hidden fear of the unknown. The Golem (1915) and 'Nosferatu' (1922) are early examples of playing off the fears of the viewers. There are countless examples of films based off of monsters, from 'King Kong' (1933) to 'Cloverfield' (2008). Disaster movies have also always rated fairly high, with such films as 'Fire!' (1901) and Armageddon (1998).

War movies are another genre that seems to always hold an audience with such films as 'All Quiet on the Western Front' (1930, 1979, and 2012) and 'Saving Private Ryan' (1998). Personal struggle and conflict is laced within every film, sometimes it feeds the story Red Dawn (1984 and 2010), other times it can be seen as character all its own, 'Army of Darkness' (1993). We can't forget the battles with alien/spiritual forces, be it from outer space, 'Independence Day' (1996) or the spirit world, 'End of Days' (1999)

The most successful films, that have the longest impact, are the films that can combine elements of our worse fears with the need to maintain our own humanity, 'Platoon' (1986) or more recently 'The Book of Eli' (2010). It is not all that hard to find such projects, 'Event Horizon' (1997). Films based on the ability to overcome heartache and rise above have always been successful, 'Lost Horizon' (1937). The ones that become cult classics are those which cross genres and mix elements of each 'I Walked with a Zombie' (1943). There are countless films which have made this transition from one genre to another, 'Undead' (2003) combined science fiction, horror, and drama.

Often the label of a particular genre may be the very key to reaping great financial rewards. Imagine a tragic romance built around a famous moment in history, 'Titanic' (1997) was the first film to gross over a billion dollars. However, it could also spell the films doom. 'Pearl Harbor' (2001), was not well received, though since it has done very well, and 'Australia' (2008), which did not fare well in American markets, are two examples of genre crossing films that put their emphasis perhaps in the wrong category.

Many will argue that any film's success or failure depends largely on the overall story, marketing, the timing of release, or who is in it. Others argue it's the budget that makes a film. Though most would say the proper combination is what makes a film a success. Look at 'The Good, the Bad, and the Ugly' (1968) it has stood the test of time and was hugely successful. The film also had a perfect mix of action, timing, characters, everything… and it truly crossed genres. It was a western, an action/adventure, a war drama, full of greed, the perfect mix and an outstanding example of mixing with various genres and sub-genres into one masterpiece.

The Zombie/Nuclear Holocaust Genre 101

We are fascinated with biology and science, viruses and the occult, war and survival, the relationship between our own mortality and what lies beyond. As man pushes forward with our Godlike experiments and studies of things perhaps better left untouched we open the doorway to our either our salvation or our own demise.

In both the Zombie and Nuclear Holocaust genres this is explored, or more correctly the result is explored... The Webster's definition may not exactly match the Hollywood definition of a zombie. But the idea of being attacked by the reanimated corpse of a loved one can be very unsettling! Holocaust and apocalypse are often interchanged and the film definition makes them one in the same. But, actually an apocalypse is a *prophecy* about a destructive event (the Book of Revelations) while, a holocaust *is* the destructive event (such as by nuclear war, or mass genocide against a group of people). We'll use the more common (Hollywood) definitions... technicalities can be such a bother...

With the idea of a Zombielike breakout, there are thousands of books/graphic novels, hundreds of movies, and even a TV series, 'The Walking Dead' (2010). Not mention the countless times they have been highlight in shows like the 'Tales from the Crypt' (1989) and music videos 'Thriller' (1983). Of course we can't forget the numerous video games as well 'Silent Hill' (2006, 2012).

The same can be said for the holocaust genre. Even before the first atom bombs fell on Japan at the end of WWII people have held a horrifying fascination with this reality. This was so ingrained in our minds throughout the Cold War days that bunkers were build in backyards, school held drills, and there were numerous protocols put in place to react to such a threat. We were so sure of blowing ourselves up that it still dictates world policies today. At one time only a handful of nations had nuclear capability (at their peak the United States had as many as 32,000 warheads and the USSR had 45,000 warheads). Now as more and more 'rogue' nations are able to become a nuclear power the reality is more evident than ever.

What the writers and creators show us is both entertaining and scary at the same time. Biological/viral outbreaks occur rather often. Outbreaks occur so often in fact that, the epidemiology profession has developed a number of widely accepted steps for investigating disease outbreaks. To see the basic outline go to the Center for Disease Control and Prevention website (www.cdc.gov). The CDC, in 2011, even created a blog warning about a zombie apocalypse:

(http://emergency.cdc.gov/socialmedia/zombies_blog.asp)

George A Romero has often been given credit as the creator of the 'Zombie' genre of films, he may have perfected it, but there were many before his. 'Revolt of the Zombies' (1936) and 'King of the Zombies' (1941) both dealt with the genre. But what Romero did do was to create the format by which almost all other Zombie films would follow. Though the zombies in newer films are more mobile, at times almost supernatural, the premise is still the same. The dead are reanimated from, a virus, 'Resident Evil' (2002, 2004, 2007, 2008, 2011), aliens, 'Plan Nine from Outer Space' (1959), government testing, 'Planet Terror' (2007) or they just exist, 'Zombie 2' (1979). Whatever the cause, they now walk among us devouring everything in their path, or turning helpless victims into the walking dead.

Keep in mind, one must not confuse the Zombie genre, 'Zombie Strippers' (2008), with the Vampire genre, 'Angel' (1999-2004), though both have similar characteristics. Zombies are reanimated corpses, they are usually mindless, primitive, and lack any real organization 'Zombie Hunters, City of The Dead' (2005-2013(?). Vampires on the other hand have a social order, are immortal, and they are intelligent, 'Twilight' (2008, 2009, 2011, 2012). The actual intelligence of a Zombie has not been properly tested, or the doctor and his/her research never survive the outbreak.

The 'Residence Evil' franchise, 'House of the Dead' (2003, 2005) and 'Doom' (2005), though all based from video games, follow the basic format. If the living dies they reanimate, they hunger for the living, and they're never full... and I guess I should add the undead ranks grow as the living shrinks. One main difference is that all living things tend to be infected humans, dogs, birds, and anything else that gets attacked. This differs from the more traditional Zombie genre, because it is usually only the humans that get infected.

There are many films that seem to have a similar format but technically are not actual 'Zombie' films. The infected are not dead, just carriers, the concept often parallels the genre. The most obvious example would be the 28 (Days, Weeks, Months) Later (2002, 2007, 2013) franchise and the more recent 'Carriers' (2009). Then of course there is 'Night of the Comet' (1984) and 'CHUD' (1984), where the attackers are not dead but mutated.

One cannot speak of this genre without giving proper credit... a lot of this genre can trace its roots to the 1954 novel 'I am Legend'. Which has spawned several movie adaptations, 'The last Man on Earth' (1964) with Vincent Price, 'The Omega Man' (1971) with Charlton Heston, and 'I am Legend' (2007) with Will Smith. Not to mention the countless movies and books which were directly influenced is blatantly obvious. So it is easy to see that when a format is found, it becomes the standard for others to follow.

The same can be said for almost any genre, when a format is found that works, most stories of a similar type will stick to what works. The romance, boy meets girls, boy loses girl, and love is found in the end, 'He Said She Said' (1991). The sports genre usually takes an underdog team and transforms it into a winner, 'Major League' (1989). Westerns have the antihero ride in not wanting to get involved but for whatever reason (love, money, vengeance...) he does and saves the day, 'Shane' (1953). The war genre follows a handful of soldiers (often green recruits), a squad of regular troops, or a special operations team assigned to accomplish some mission and their struggles, 'The Big Red One' (1980).

But as mentioned before the greatest films that stand the test of time are those who break the rules. But also can find a way to combine elements of other genres, 'Deadbirds' (2004). These are movies that makes one almost root for the bad guy, 'Road to Perdition' (2002). Often can make one want to know what lies ahead, what hardship must our main character endure, or ask why this is happening, 'Blade Runner' (1982).

Often we are intrigued with the ultimate test of survival, 'Cast Away' (2000). Whether the test is against natural elements, 'The Submersion of Japan' (1973) or nature itself 'Tarantula' (1955) we are want to see how the story plays out. Although there are tons of such stories, the ones that keep us coming back for more often pits 'man' against his own humanity, 'The Ninth Configuration' (1980).

Of this genre none capture the imagination more than the apocalyptic holocaust, 'Panic in Year Zero' (1962). There is a deep need to see the future after the final war of all wars, 'A Boy and his Dog' (1975). Watching this surreal world as it unfolds before us, we see people who were ripped from the normal life into a living hell, 'The Day After' (1983). Then we get to see how they build order out of chaos to live again, 'The Postman' (1997).

The dread of an unknown future in a world filled with more ways to destroy than to create has inspired a long list of post apocalyptic films, from H.G. Wells 'Things to Come' (1936) to "When the Wind Blows' (1986) to '20 Years After' (2008). We have a deep thirst for human struggle and coming to terms with a bleak future, 'Testament' (1983). The viewer gets to see the various creations of a world gone mad and how the survivors cope, 'Radioactive Dreams' (1985).

Often times in this new reality are found hidden dangers which give the creators the freedom to expand on the genre, 'World Without End' (1956). They may have to deal with the harsh climate and the effects that the fallout has had on the environment, 'Damnation Alley' (1977). Perhaps the apocalypse has created a whole new set of adversaries, 'Hell comes to Frogtown' (1987).

The master of this new found reality is George Miller. He created a world gone mad after a not to clear holocaustic apocalypse occurred. From ancient times until now, we have feared a future based in the unknown, 'Planet of the Apes' (1968). Though Miller didn't create the genre, he helped to mold a format for others to copy and follow, 'The Bronx Warriors' (1983) and 'The New Barbarians' (1982) are just two such examples.

Often the genre will be mixed with elements of other genres, the western is a common focus, 'Deadly Reactor' (1989). Sometimes there is a mix of fantasy, 'Warriors of the Apocalypse' (1985). But all follow a base format consisting of bands of people huddled together, fighting a group of marauders and a hero(s) to save the day, '2019, After the Fall of New York' (1983).

Usually the hero is someone thrust in to that position due to circumstance, accident, or other personal reasons, 'The Aftermath' (1982). Sometimes the heroes are a mixed matched group just trying to carve out a basic existence, 'The Blood of Heroes' (1989). Other times it is a case of being at the wrong place at the wrong time, 'Creepozoids' (1987). Whatever the reason the viewer wants to see how they will survive in this strange yet familiar world of the post-apocalyptic future.

The end of the world, holocaust, total destruction, and the willingness of man to prevail is nothing new. History is full of such tales of woe. Almost every culture has myths and legends which touch on the topic. Whether it's Biblical, the story of Atlantis, or the Mayan calendar we are glued to the idea. Then like cockroaches we return to reclaim our rightful place as head of the food chain, once again dominating the planet.

No one seems to show this better than George A Romero and George Miller. After everything is lost and all hope should be gone…

"We will rebuild", Aunty (Beyond Thunderdome).

George A Romero/George Miller Genre Intro

Though I gave a brief introduction to the genres, the intention of this writing is as a respectful tribute to two filmmakers whose combined talents recreated two genres for future filmmakers to emulate. These men need no introduction to their true fans. George A Romero has been a writer, producer, and director and is most famous for his development of the 'Zombie' genre. George Miller is also a writer, producer, and director and often associated with the 'Mad Max' post-apocalyptic genre.

Their efforts, though may not have been intentional, have created entire new 'universes' where our deepest, darkest, and most savage primal nightmares clash the very essence of what it means to be human. The characters are torn from what is their normal 'environment' and trust into a world of chaos. In their recreation of reality is found a very real parallel to the actual world we live in. The demons may be of fiction but the outcome and the examples of man's own destructive tendencies are all too real.

Though these films were made on separate continents, a full decade apart initially, they live on and in fact are now a part of our very culture. But there is more to these stories then the mere impact they have had on the cinema, the countless copycat productions, and marketing gimmicks over the years. They are, in fact, in depth look at the very soul of what it means to be human.

Now of course there have been several knock offs but none top the George A Romero universe. He takes normal everyday people and thrust them into a living nightmare. Creating a world that gives a new meaning to the survival of the fittest. He explores both the social impact and personal/emotional stress of surviving this hell on earth.

As for George Miller's world of Mad Max, we have only had cheap imitations to dine on while waiting for the master to return to the genre. Though his was not the first to deal with life after a holocaust, it was by far the greatest and created a mythological like world following the destruction of society. It has been a long time, too long though since Max entered the world, and there have been too many cheap imitations.

These two genres might very well go hand in hand. In fact it can be argued that they are more than powerful visions but, are actually a true example of cause and effect. The idea that you can't have one without the other, building on the myth, and creating a deep underlining story which is simply... man can overcome. The two story lines may have actually taken place in the same universe, a parallel time-line to our own yet not independent of each other. The concept may in fact seem outlandish at first until one takes the time to analyze the sometimes subtle connections.

Though this may seem like a wild conspiracy theory, up there with JFK, Roswell, and 911 but, once you have reviewed the facts and see for yourself the pattern of interlocking clues, you will come to the same undeniable conclusion. Once one takes the time to break down the stories, it is clearly reveled what the truth is behind the holocaust, the fall of society, and the rebirth of the cities. George Romero set up the fall of society with his first masterpiece and George Miller explained what would be the lasting result on the survivors.

Now it is the intention of this essay to point out many of the key points and interlocking pieces of the puzzle that connect the two stories into one mythology. Just like the stories from ancient legends are not stand alone stories but are fragments of a greater story. Those ancient myths often are connected with other stories which build upon one another. If one takes the time to read the stories left behind from the ancient Greeks, Babylonians, and other past cultures it is easy to see how they build on each other. The same can be said for these two genres.

The connection may or may not be obvious to the untrained observer. But if one takes the time to watch the films, in order of release you will see how the two intertwine into one saga of the total destruction of 'civilization' and the growing attempts to build back. One of the roots of both is the internal instinct to survive. All creatures are born with the basic instincts, everything else is learned behavior.

Now for those who may not be as familiar with the overall time line of the two story lines I will give a brief synopsis of each film in question. Then in the following chapters the stories will be looked at in fuller detail. Keep in mind the universe in which these events take place is not our own but a parallel timeline.

Night of the Living Dead:

It is 1968 when the dead first rise and attack the living. Though at first it is not clear what is happening the scientific experts at the time believe that this nightmare was cause by radioactive fallout from a space probe that exploded high in the Earth's atmosphere. The story follows a small group of survivors shortly after this incident. They are hiding out in an old farm house. The only working vehicle is out of gas and a large horde of murderous lunatics stand between them and the farm's fuel storage tank. All the information is obtained through television and radio reports. That is how we learn of the nature of the attackers and the best defense against them, 'gunshot or heavy blow to the head'. The story ends with armed vigilantly/posse groups hunting down the undead.

Dawn of the dead:

It is 1978 society is in the final stage of collapsing, martial law is in effect. The military, law enforcement, and civilian vigilantes are combing the country side hunting for the undead. Cities are becoming deathtraps as the reanimated dead consume the living. There are many who refuse to accept the fact that their dead relatives are nothing more than ghouls and refuse to follow lawful directives to surrender all undead to the proper authorities. As the story progresses it becomes clear that the government has lost control and that the outbreak is too widespread to be stopped. With a helicopter, a handful of survivors, seeing the end is near, head north to the wilderness of Canada but, instead end up in a shopping mall, due to the lack of fuel. Not only must they contend with the 'zombies' they must also fight marauders who come and raid for food and supplies as now it is becoming everyone for themselves.

Mad Max:

It is 1979/80. After the holocaust, when the nations of world resorted to nuclear attacks. Small communities are still trying to survive even though the major cities have been destroyed and the governments are either dissolved or in hiding. Max Rockatansky is a survivor from the earlier holocaust, a cop and a family man. The community which he lives in is trying to rebuild itself and one of his duties is to protect the citizens from the roaming bands of gangs and marauders. As it gets more and more personal between the marauders and the police Max decides to leave the force. But, before he can find his peace, the gang attacks his family, he 'snaps' and hunts down the gang, taking him into the wasteland.

The Road Warrior (Mad Max2):

The years melt into each other, society has completely collapsed by now. But there are those who still hold on to the hope of a brighter future, this small band of well wishers are in possession of a working oil refinery. They have hopes of refining enough fuel to take them two thousand miles north to a safe haven they affectionately call 'paradise'. The marauders are running out of places to go and are in need of fuel. They surround the refinery and battle for the fuel within. Max just wants a full tank and chance to move on but, gets caught up in the middle of this conflict. He reluctantly assists in the daring breakout, through the surrounding band of marauders, and off to 'paradise'. The trick works but he is again left alone…

The Day of the Dead:

Just before the final collapse, organized government teams of scientist were dispatched to secure and safe locations. Their goal was simple, find a cure or find a way to combat this plague. As time passes the survivors steadily realize the reality of the situation. With communications lost, no new survivors being found, and a lack of viable solutions the military commander grows more impatient. Discipline is steadily lost and self preservation becomes priority. This soon pits the soldiers against the civilian doctors. Like everywhere else on the planet, the small group soon turns on themselves. The only hope is to fly to a safe isolated place. But first they must compete against each other before combating the army of undead which awaits their next meal...

Mad Max Beyond Thunderdome:

Long since the fall of society we find Max travelling across the wasteland. In this new world of man against man he loses everything. In an attempt to get it back he goes to 'Bartertown', just one example of the many attempts at recreating society. In this surreal community he strikes a deal, remove one of the obstacles in Aunty's attempt at total control and he can get his stuff back. The deal doesn't work out as planned and he is banished to the desert wasteland. There he is found by a group of children, survivors of a plane crash, a futile attempt to save them from the holocaust. Max gets caught up helping them, taking on Aunty's army of marauders, and finding his own humanity.

Land of the Dead:

The actual year is unknown, though it is at least thirty to forty years after the initial outbreak. Society has found a way of rebuilding. There is a sense of normal. The survivors have taken a small city, sealed it off, and created a place where they can live again. The powerful live large, while the rest of the community must work to keep everything operational, in this new city. The marauders are more organized, better equipped. There are two overlaying storylines. The first follows up on the idea that the undead can relearn and 'evolve' at a basic level. The second is the struggle of survival and one's own humanity.

Other films/sequels

There are also several parallel stories that go along with these. 'Diary of the Dead' follows a separate group during what is suppose to be the original outbreak and their attempt to come to terms with what is happening. The other story is 'Survival of the Dead', which again is a parallel story following a group of researchers working to find a cure while dealing with the attackers.

Of course one cannot forget the remake of 'Dawn of the Dead' (2004). Though most will agree it is not so much a remake as a parallel storyline. It is not unlikely that others would find sanctuary in a shopping mall. When one watches the two films it is clear that they are suppose to take place in the same timeframe, ignoring that it is updated and uses modern technology. It actually supports the other films quite well.

As of this writing the long awaited 'Mad Max 4' is scheduled to be produced, possibly 2012. At this time there is no further information… and of course anything is possible.

The connection will be draw from the above mentioned seven films, as the others are supporting and MM4 has yet to be released. First I will present a fuller description of the stories, followed by key plot points that help link them into one mythology. Finally I will give a short linkage showing how all the pieces fit together. For those who have a need to remember the dead, the last section is dedicated to loss of life. Just some random stats from past disasters, plagues, and wars.

SECTION II

-The Films-

The Night of the Living Dead (1968)

Dawn of the Dead (1978)

Mad Max (1979)

Mad Max 2: The Road Warrior (1981)

Day of the Dead (1985)

Mad Max Beyond Thunderdome (1985)

Land of the Dead (2005)

Night of the Living Dead (1968)

'Pits the dead against the living in a struggle for survival!'

The story begins with a long drive down an isolated road. In the car is Johnny and Barbra (brother and sister), Johnny wears black and leather driving gloves. They finally arrive to the cemetery to visit the grave of a lost loved one. While there they are attacked and Johnny gets killed. Barbra makes it to the car but Johnny has the keys. Putting the car in neutral she manages to coast away. When she can no longer use the car she runs to a nearby farm house, resting on a fuel pump before making her way into the house.

Inside is Ben another survivor of the attack. He was at a diner when the attacks started. The assailants were attacking a fuel tanker truck. He took a truck, drove away, and ended up at that farm house. The truck was almost out of gas. The only weapon he had was a tire iron.

After fending off another attack Ben realizes the seriousness of the situation. He learns that fire is one of his main weapons against these attackers. He begins to figure out a way to barricade the house. While Barbra helps to look for boards and such she notices a music box which she plays. Together they work to board up and secure the windows and doors.

Once that is done he finds a radio. The announcer speaks of an epidemic of mass murder, what government actions are being taken, mass panic, to stay off the streets and such reports. The station also reports of rescue stations being setup by the law enforcement and National Guard. There are not any real explanations as to what is causing this. One theory leans towards fallout from a returning Venus probe, which was destroyed in the upper atmosphere for carrying a strange radiation.

It is soon reveled that hiding in the basement were several other survivors. Among them are Tom, his girlfriend Judy, the Coopers, and their daughter. The young girl has been bitten and is very sick. They had been attacked on the road and managed to find their way to this house. Ben and Judy are from the area and know their way around.

In the house Ben has found one rifle and a few shells. There is a lot of tension between the main characters. Ben, the self appointed leader, is determined to find a way out. It is decided that they can get the truck to the gas pump. Molotov cocktails are made and thrown from the upstairs windows to allow for Ben and Tom to get to the truck. Judy refuses to be left behind and they make their way through the attackers to the pump. But the truck catches fire and is destroyed. Tom and Judy are killed in the process.

The Cooper's daughter 'dies' and 'awakens'. Ben and Mr. Cooper fight for the rifle and Cooper is killed. Other undead make their way into the house. In the basement Mrs. Cooper is attacked by her own child. Ben makes his way to the basement, finishes off any undead there and waits for the rescuers to arrive.

The local and state law enforcement agencies are combing the area, killing off any undead. The plan is to meet up with the National Guard. Along with them are the news media and a civilian posse armed with rifles and shotguns. They eventually make their way to the farmhouse.

Common links:

The use of desolate roads, lone vehicles, and chases involving the vehicle

Johnny wears black and driving gloves

The theme of finding a strong hold and debating to stay or run

The small music box

Radiation fallout, from a satellite, is the possible cause

Ben was at a small diner when he witnessed attacks

Fuel is a major factor, complete with fuel trucks and gas pumps. There is an ongoing need for fuel

Tom, dark haired, is a 'driver'

Zombies grab at their prey

They use fire as a weapon

The posse uses revolvers and shotguns

They have helicopters

Use dogs to help fight of attackers

Dawn of the Dead (1978)

'When there's no more room in hell, the dead will walk the earth.'

The story begins about ten years after the initial outbreak. There has been a steady loss of social order. Martial law has been declared. The police, military, and local organizations are still combating the horde of undead. It is highly debated as to the cause of this outbreak and to the proper course of action that needs to be taken.

A lawful decree has been issued and the authorities have ordered the collection of the deceased, though many refuse to accept that their loved ones are truly nothing more than soulless creatures. The police conduct raids on various housing units in search of the undead. There are those who fight against the police. The dead are destroyed and the bodies are to be collected.

As this roundup progresses, many of the living go berserk and kill anything in their path. Command and control is steadily lost. One can see a breakdown of even the multi-media outlets, leadership, and society as a whole. It becomes apparent that the city will soon fall as the authority is lost and the undead continue to grow in numbers.

Several of the police officers decide to go. Some find different means of escaping, after looting for needed supplies. Others take the helicopter from the local news station and fly out of the city. They need to try and avoid the military and other agencies but, still need fuel. They decide to head north.

As they are traveling they see the armed gangs hunting after the undead. Once the dead are neutralized the bodies are burned. But they seem unstoppable. They continue to travel avoiding major population only landing to rest, refuel, and resupply.

Finally the need for rest overpowers the need to flee and they land on the roof of a shopping mall. After much debate they decided to stay. First they must remove the undead from inside the mall then secure it from other survivors who may fight for the supplies inside. They use semi-trucks to block the doors, build a 'safe-room', and use the heating/air conditioning ducts to travel.

While safe inside, they are able to watch news reports. At first these reports are well organized and professional but as time goes by the chaos overwhelms the country. The televised reports show a steady decline in society, debates on what should be the proper course of action, and what the long term effects are. The powers that be debate the use of nuclear arms and the abandonment of the major cities.

While in the mall they loot the various stores as needed and take everything back to their 'safe room'. They use mannequins for target practice. The parking lot continues to fill with the undead as they want to get into the mall.

Meanwhile, and unbeknownst to them, they are being watched by leather clad Marauders. An organized gang of bikers and other survivors looking to loot and take what they can from the mall. From a safe point they watch trying to make a plan of attack.

Various weapons are used in the attack, guns, bows/arrows, axes and other such primitive weapons as the marauders attack and break into the mall. The gang takes whatever they can from guns and ammo to clothes and boots.

The police officers and the pilot try to fight off the gang. They continue to use the ducts and even shoot out through the vents in an attempt to stop the marauders from taking everything. Unfortunately the mall is also filled with the undead and everyone needs to go. The gang goes back out the way they came in as the others make their way to the roof.

They make a final stand before getting airborne and fly off.

Common Links:

The police officers being key characters

Use of a helicopter

Ongoing need for fuel

Use of shotguns and revolvers

Use of mannequin

Use of view finder

Leather clad bikers/marauders

One of the police officers is an expert driver

Use of semi truck

Need to head north (to a safe area)

Use of fire to cremate the remains

Use of primitive weapons

Use of air ducts

The use of the nuclear option was described

Mad Max (1979)...

'The last law in a world gone out of control.
Pray that he's out there somewhere.'

This is after the fall of society. It is not clearly stated what has happened, though several references are made to lead the viewer to the conclusion that this is after a worldwide holocaust. This community is trying to rebuild itself and move forward with life.

The streets are overrun with marauders and gangs who combat the limited resources of the local police. The police are clad in leather protective uniforms. They work from the looted police station to track down criminals to try and maintain some sense of law and order.

The roads have become battlefields as people fight to survive. A road sign is even shown to emphasize this, "High fatality road-deaths this year-57". The dispatcher can be heard giving various bits of information and warnings such as "do not cross territorial range" and "Prohibited area".

It all starts out with the pursuit of an escaped convict driving a stolen police 'special'. He is a biker who has been labeled a 'terminal suicide'. The police are in pursuit hoping to catch him before he makes his way into the populated areas, where society has begun to rebuild itself.

The officers are in pursuit while Max gets ready to join the chase. He asks about damage after a pursuit vehicle crashes. The Nightrider says "you should see the damage, metal damage, brain damage..." He then starts to think of the world that was, crying about how "nothing is left…it's all gone"

After the Nightrider is killed in a crash Max returns to his home, he has a wife and child. She plays the saxophone, one can see they are the normal loving couple. The TV reports about another officer being killed, it is implied that this fragile community is on the verge of collapse along with the rest of society. Max uses a zombie mask to tease with his wife… but he must go off to work.

Max works the scene of a car crash. The police are wrapping up, clearing the scene. They talk of it being a couple of "crazies". Some victims are seen still moving about.

Meanwhile the biker gang enters a small town to collect the remains of the Nightrider. They harass the townspeople, take what they want. They chase after a car, destroying it before attacking and raping the occupants.

Max and Goose arrive at the scene, Johnny is still there and he is "wacked out of his skull". He is taken into custody the female victim is taken for medical treatment. The gang sends Bubba to retrieve Johnny.

Another failed attempt at restoring law and order, no one shows up for the trial. Words are shared. Johnny is free to go, and says "see you later Goose", and smacks the back of his skull.

The biker gang is out on the beach, Bubba is about to do some target practice on a mannequin. Before he can fire Johnny grabs a shotgun and shoots it in the head. Toecutter drags him to water, threatening to blow his head off. The gang then regroups.

It is announced that there is a curfew in effect, the streets are deserted. Goose's police motorcycle is seen outside in a parking area, where it gets sabotaged. Goose is at a club and he picks up a singer with which he spends the night with. The next day he out patrolling, when his bike malfunctions and he wrecks. He is able to walk back and get a truck. As he is driving back when Johnny throws an object into the windshield causing the vehicle to wreck. The truck is upside down and leaking fuel, Toecutter and Johnny arrive, after a bit of pressure Johnny throws a match and Goose burns while trapped in the truck.

Max arrives at the hospital and goes to the Goose's room. He is horrified by what he sees. He tells his commander "that thing in there is not the Goose". That night Max has a bad nightmare. He talks with his wife about how full of life the Goose was. Later Max decides to resign from the force. His commander tries to give him the 'hero' speech. Max calls it the "mad circus" and he is afraid of becoming one of them, 'a terminal crazy'.

Max and his family pack up go for a trip along the coast. He spends some much needed quality time with his wife and son. He speaks of his father and his shiny brown shoes, taking long strides as he walked. Max also speaks of how he regrets not telling his father how he felt when he had the chance.

Later they drive to a mechanic to get a tire fixed. Max stays behind as his wife goes up the road for some ice cream. There she runs into the Toecutter and his gang of marauders. They tease of having a meal... she manages to get away. Max and she drive off to a safer place.

Toecutter questions the mechanic who says they are heading north (maybe). The mechanic speaking to himself speaks of how "the world is full of crazy people". The gang silently pursuits Max, following him up the coast. They finally track him down to where he and his family are staying. Which happens to be with the family of a fellow police officer, from another territory.

Max is warned of possible trouble, takes his shotgun, and goes to see for himself while he is gone the gang attacks his wife and son. Though she tried to get away, the bikers run her down. Later at the hospital Max listens as the list off all the injuries his family received from the attack. The nurse states how he is just standing there "like a zombie".

Max goes home and tries to come to terms with what has happened to his family. In his anger he tears up the zombie mask. Finally he snaps and goes into his home puts on his uniform returns to the station and steals his pursuit special police car. He then goes on the hunt killing off the biker gang one by one.

To do so he must enter the area clearly marked as the 'Prohibited Area'. He stalks some of the bikers as they siphon fuel from a tanker truck. When Max finds Johnny he is at the scene of a car crash. Johnny screams "you can't kill me… he was dead already". Max handcuffs Johnny's leg to the car and drives off.

Common Links:

Takes place after an unexplained holocaust

Main characters are both police officers and marauders

The use of shotguns and revolvers

Fuel tanker truck

Mannequins

Fire and dogs

References (the zombie mask, him standing like a zombie)

Leather clad bikers and officers

Traveling north (safer place)

People live in protected areas

Experienced drivers, driving gloves

Desolate roads and car chases

Max's wife plays the saxophone

Mad Max 2: The Road Warrior (1981)

'In the future, cities will become deserts, roads will become battlefields and the hope of mankind will appear as a stranger.'

The story begins with these words; "My life fades, all that remains are memories... I remember a time of chaos. Gone now, two warriors tribes went to war. Leaders talked but nothing could stem the avalanche, their world crumbled, cities exploded... a firestorm of fear. Men began to feed on men. Only those mobile enough would survive..."

A few years have gone by since Max snapped after the loss of his family. He is now a lonely drifter wandering the prohibited areas in search of supplies, fuel, and his own humanity. His only companion is a dog.

People have become primitive and savage. They wear makeshift armor, have altered their vehicles for defense, and use cross bows/arrows as bullets have become scarce. They are more nomadic in nature and tribal.

Max is chased by a small band of marauders. They want his fuel and anything else he may have. Max manages to outdrive them and after a vehicle wrecks he takes the fuel. He is at the crash site of a semi truck that had previously been overpowered by marauders. On the side of the truck it is written 'the vermin are everywhere'. As max checks out the vehicle he finds a small music box.

Max continues on still in need of fuel. He stumbles upon a gyrocopter, as he tries to grab a snake that is on the vehicle the pilot appears from his hiding place. Thinking he has Max and his vehicle the pilot is attacked by Max's dog. A deal is struck as to where Max can get fuel. There is a working refinery which is the home of a more peaceful group of people.

The refinery, however, is surrounded by the marauders, who are encamped and trying to get the fuel. Almost daily they attack the refinery trying to find a way in. At the same time, the people within are trying to find a means of escape. Max observes this from a safe advantage point, with the gyro pilot chained to a log. They had a deal, Max says the deal was he wouldn't kill him.

The people in the refinery have a system of flame-throwers and harpoon style weapons as well as crossbows and compound bows for defense. Which they successfully repel the attacks. The marauders are armed with similar weapons as well as gas powered dart guns. Most everyone wears heavy layers of clothing, leather, and pads for protection.

The marauders have fixed up hot-rod cars, motorcycles, tow-trucks, former police cars, and anything they can use for transport. Those inside the refinery have limited vehicles but they still attempt to break out and find a means to escape. Max seeing the dilemma waits for an opportunity to present itself.

An opportunity does arise when the marauders attack an escaping vehicle, the marauders rape and attempt to kill the drivers just as Max arrives. He strikes a deal with one of the survivors, fuel for the man's life. He makes his way to the refinery but before he can cash in on his deal the man dies.

They call Max "a parasite trading in human flesh" and take him prisoner (the people of the refinery don't know what to do with him). The marauders return with the prisoners tied to their vehicles. The feral kid kills one of the gang with a boomerang. Humongous understands the pain "we all lost someone we love". "There has been too much violence, too much pain". He tells them to just walk away.

Max listens as the group discusses what to do. Should they give up or fight or run... But the tanker is their lifeline to a new life, 2000 miles north. As Max listens, the feral kid pops out of a hole, Max gives him the music box. He then makes a new deal. He agrees to get a truck big enough to haul their fuel tanker, in return for his vehicle and all the fuel he can carry. They agree and he sets off with enough fuel to return with the truck.

Along the way he stumbles across the gyro pilot, who is still chained to the log. Max makes him carry the fuel cans. As they walk the pilot speaks of things from the past, all the things he misses such as lingerie. Finally they reach the gyrocopter. After flying to the truck, max gets it started. He drives to the refinery while the gyrocopter flies overhead.

The marauders try to stop him, attacking the truck. Even Humungous uses a couple of his last remaining bullets. But Max manages to get to through and safe inside the refinery. The pilot lands inside as well. After a quick survey the truck can be repaired and used to haul the tanker.

Humongous is furious about the truck and sets a couple of the prisoners on fire. He rallies his men and tells the refinery that none of them will make it out alive. During this time they repair the truck and get themselves ready to leave. The Gyro pilot tries to convince a young girl to leave with him saying "it will be safer up there".

Meanwhile max checks and fuels his aging pursuit special. They try to talk him into staying to drive the tanker. He is told of the need to build a future and how together they can rebuild their lives. All they have to do is make it two thousand miles to paradise, "nothing to do but breed". Max however, has other plans. He is called a "maggot living in the corpse of the old world". He is asked "what burned him out? Kill one too many, see too many people die?" He is reminded that they all lived through it. They are still human beings but Max belongs out there with the "garbage".

With that Max leaves. He is noticed though when he goes and some of the marauders chase after him. They catch up with him and cause him to lose control and wreck his car. The marauders try to steal his fuel but his tanks are booby trapped and blow when tampered with. The smoke is seen from the refinery and the gyrocopter pilot goes to the rescue.

After this Max has no choice but to make a new deal. He will now drive the tanker truck. Everyone loads up and makes their getaway. Most of the marauders chase after the fuel tanker. Some enter into the refinery, which has been rigged with explosives and blows up. Leaving both groups with no option but to either get or keep control of the tanker truck.

Max finds out when it is too late that he was just a decoy. The tanker was filled with sand the fuel was placed in barrels and went with the main group. The main group heads north with the gyro pilot.

Common Links:

Narration and conversations about the state of the world

World holocaust explained (possible nuclear)

Use of fire and dogs

Primitive weapons

Shotgun and revolver

Need for fuel/Fuel tanker truck

Pilot

Leather clad people

Armored vehicles/police cars

Desolate roads and car chases

Max still has tattered driving gloves

Travelling north

The Day of the Dead (1985)

'The Dead have waited. The day has come.'

This is now some years later, after the dead have taken over. Most people deserted the cities. Though there is still hope of survivors. A group of researchers fly a helicopter into one of the now deserted cities. It is soon realized that the only things still occupying the town is the walking dead. They quickly leave and fly back to their base.

The base has two main sections. The above ground section is fenced in and is mainly for the helipad, fuel, and a small 'garden' (with hordes of the undead stopped only by a chain linked fence). While the main section of the base camp is an old underground storage bunker, which has been converted into a research facility. It is divided into several areas, the research labs, the living area, storage, and holding area (for the undead being used as 'lab rats'). The primary entrance is an electronic elevating platform.

The soldiers and civilians maintain a noticeable degree of separation, even living in different areas of the compound. The military and civilian researchers clearly have differing views on the purpose of the facility and how to handle the problem at hand. Communications with 'higher command' has long ceased and it is clear that the undead are ruling the world.

Command and control is breaking down as everyone tries to come to terms with what has happened. With the loss of the recent commander the overly zealous Captain assumes command. He demands results from the civilian doctors who are performing experiments on captured zombies. It is discovered that the undead can live for years as long the brain remains intact.

One of the researchers/doctors is dubbed 'Frankenstein' due to the nature of his work/experiments. He has come to the conclusion that rather than trying to find a weapon to destroy them they should try to domesticate them. The Captain strongly disagrees and dislikes what he sees so far. There is a clear division between the belief that the undead should be destroyed and the belief that they can be trained.

Frankenstein tries to prove his theory by demonstrating the 'intelligence' of his pet. The pet shows residual memories of prior military service when it attempts to salute the Captain. He also has the ability to relearn basic tasks.

The soldiers risk their lives by collecting 'samples' for study. It is soon discovered just how mentally unstable Frankenstein is. He uses the soldiers that had fallen victim to the virus for his experiments and as food for his test subjects.

When the Captain discovers this he snaps and decides it is time to take full control of the operation and to eliminate the civilians. After killing Frankenstein he takes the civilians prisoner and throws them into the holding area, with the undead. He is ready to get out of there and take his men with him in hopes of finding somewhere safe, the 'promised land'.

The base eventually gets overrun with the undead. It soon becomes a situation where everyone is fending for themselves. Frankenstein's pet makes his way around the base ultimately killing the Captain (with a handgun).

The remaining survivors make their way to the top and find the area crawling with undead. The gate is open and they are pouring in. The fight is on for them to get to the helicopter and get out…

Common links:

Barren empty streets

Use of helicopter

The need for fuel

Use of revolvers and other guns

Fortified compound

Use of a loud speaker

Music (the tape recorder)

The vehicles in storage

Mad Max Beyond Thunderdome (1985)

'A lone warrior searching for his destiny...a tribe of lost children waiting for a hero...in a world battling to survive, they face a woman determined to rule.'

Sometime has passed since last we saw Max. He is getting older. Max is still the loner traveling the wasteland in search of fuel, food, perhaps even salvation. He has acquired a new vehicle, though presumed out of fuel due to its being pulled by a team of camels.

As he moves along, silently above an airplane glides in and knocks him off the truck. The plane's engines start and it flies off as one of the pilots take control of the truck and they both head off leaving Max behind. The only friend Max has is a monkey, it throws a bunch of junk off the back of the truck, which Max collects as he tracks his vehicle.

Max follows the trail to a 'new' city... Bartertown, people from all over come to this place to trade, work, and socialize. Many wear the 'uniforms' of their former lives while other are dressed in leather and protective pads. There is a clear distinction between the regular visitor and the 'protective' guards of the city.

As Max approaches the entrance a water vender peddles up and offers water. Max tests it for radiation, which it is contaminated. The vender laughs and says "what's a little fallout"? He then rides off.

When Max enters the city he quickly proves the only thing he has to barter with is his skills. They have him leave his weapons at the entrance. He is then escorted up to Aunty's residence, which is a nice place (relative to the current environment) high above the city. There he sees a man playing the saxophone (reminiscent of his wife). Max is offered something to drink and eat. As he attempts to partake, he has his skills put to the test.

Once he passes the 'audition' they make a deal. Max is to eliminate Aunties' competition in return he gets his vehicle, camels, fuel, supplies, and other such necessities, or death if he should fail. Max learns that Bartertown is made of two parts, the above ground area where most everyone conducts business and lives, and the underworld where pigs are used to make methane (which is converted into fuel). Aunty wishes to run both.

The one he is to eliminate is in fact a team, Master-Blaster. Master is the brains and Blaster is the muscle. They tell him to keep the brain and dump the body. To do this he must try and get close them by working in the methane plant.

Per the rules of Bartertown Max waits for an opportunity to challenge Master-Blaster. Finally the moment arrives when Master-Blaster is driving Max's vehicle. A challenge is made and accepted. A fight to the death in Thunderdome… "Two men enter… one man leaves", the crowd chants. Max fights and wins but, finds himself unable to deliver the final blow.

He is accused of not completing the contract. "Bust a deal… face the wheel", judgment is passed. Max is sentence to die out in the desert, tied to a horse with no water. Through chance he manages to free himself and try to find a way out.

After he collapses Max is found by tribal girl and brought to the 'tribes' home. There he is cared for, cleaned up, his hair is cut, and they wait for him to wake. When he finally does it is as if from a nightmare.

Max learns that this tribe is actually survivors from a plane crash. A group of people took to the sky and flew away in hope of finding someplace safe. But the airplane experienced mechanical problems and crashed in the desert. After finding this place as a temporary safe haven the adults ventured out into the desert in search of rescue.

The children mistakenly think Max is the pilot, Captain Walker, and he has returned to take them back to "tomorrow morrow land". They tell the story of the past with the use of a view finder, old pictures, drawings on the wall, and an in-depth (though very skewed) narration. They speak of Mr. Death chasing them.

They are saddened when it is revealed that he is not Captain Walker. The older ones debate and some decide to trek out and find their way back. Others remind them "that when you finded him he was half jumped by Mr. Death." But the group decides to go anyway. Max is asked to stop them. He uses what they thought to be a spear but is actually an old rifle to get their attention. Max explains that he is not Captain Walker and that he "keeps Mr. Death in his pocket". He then further explains what awaits them if they leave… first of the desert but worse… Bartertown.

While he sleeps a small band leaves anyway. Max is coaxed into following out after them, which he does. After a dangerous trek across the desert they finally reach Bartertown. The children are amazed by the electric lights. Using the system of duct works they enter and make their way through the Underworld. Max finds Master and frees him just as Aunty's' soldiers charge in after them.

Using Master's vehicle they take off following the old rail line. As they do Bartertown goes up in smoke and chaos ensues but, Aunty rallies the townspeople to chase after them, with hopes of getting Master back to rebuild.

They are almost free when they come to a blockade on the tracks. There stands a boy armed, "Anybody move and you're dead meat!" He then looks past the vehicle and sees Aunty's troops closing in… "We're dead meat!" He runs off and Max, Master, and the kids pursue him through a set of tunnels to the home of the pilot.

Max convinces the pilot it would be in his best interest to fly them all out to safety. The plane is heavy and they must dump some cargo and still the plane stops… Max asks what's wrong. And the pilot says they don't have enough room. Max looks out across the vast flat desert floor questioning this statement. "Between us and them… we don't have enough room". Aunty closes in. "There will be", and with that Max takes a vehicle and charges right into Aunty's vehicles clearing a path. He is left alone… again… as the plane flies off to "Tomorrow morrow land".

Common links:

Vast isolated places

Secured compounds

The on-going need for fuel

Armored vehicles

Wearing of leather and protective clothing

Shotguns and other firearms

Use of primitive weapons

Use of pilot/aircraft

Use of a loud speaker

Use of viewfinder

Narration and conversations about the state of the world

World holocaust described (nuclear)

Use of fire and dogs

Desolate roads and car chases

Travelling north or to a better place

Land of the Dead (2005)

'The dead shall inherit the Earth.'

A lot of time has passed since the original outbreak, several decades actually. Society has found a way to rebuild. Though not explained, it is perceived that after a hard fight the survivors were able to reclaim and rebuild the mostly intact section of a large city, Pittsburgh, Pennsylvania. The city is protected on three sides by a river(s) and electric fencing along the other side.

There in this fortified city they have managed to carve out a new life... though, as with any major society, theirs is riddled with crime, black marketing, and a true distinction between the haves and the have nots. This new society is very reminiscent of the old feudal system. Kaufman runs this city with an iron fist, living high in Fiddler's Green, the coveted high-rise for the pampered few, while the majority barely exists in the slums which surround it.

We are given a more in-depth look at the marauders who scavenge the various towns looking for anything useful or considered to be of value. The items range from medical supplies and food to alcohol, something that is considered quite valuable on the black market. The marauders are better equipped and more organized. They enter the various infested towns at night launching fireworks from armored trucks. This trick creates a temporary distraction by getting the attention of the undead, making them easy targets and clearing the way.

Various teams break off and collect what is needed. They use motorcycles, converted and armed vehicles, and have even designed a special vehicle called Dead Reckoning. The colossus armored truck is almost like a tank complete with rockets. It is state of the art in its design.

As the marauders raid through the town they eliminate many of the undead. However, as stated earlier the primary objective is to collect as much supplies, food, and medicines as possible. This is all collected with the idea that it gets redistributed among the residents of the 'living' city. There are those who have more personal agendas, they collect things that have a high value in the black market.

Riley has been on several of these runs and he has plans to take a car and head north. This is to be his last raid into the neighboring towns looking for supplies. Cholo, a hot-head, is to assume command of the raiding party. He has already been enforcing Kaufman's personal agendas... He now has other ideas, delusions of living in Fiddler's Green, the center of the city where all the wealthy and powerful live in ultra-modern luxury. As stated, Fiddler's Green is in stark contrast to the dilapidated areas the rest of the citizens live.

With little incident they make their way back to the city. Unknown to them is that the Zombies tend to revert back to their most basic self. Prior to this they all had lives and the zombies seem to have reverted to this. The gas station attendant still works his station, a brass band still hold on to their instruments, lovers even still walk hand in hand. But more than this they seem to have developed basic intelligence, they communicate with each other and have relearned some problem solving skills to the point of using tools and weapons...

Everyone celebrates another successful raid. Cholo goes to Kaufman to announce his moving up in the world only to find out that he really means nothing to Kaufman, he is nothing more than a tool. Cholo now makes a decision to turn on Kaufman.

Meanwhile Riley tries makes his way around visiting friends and getting ready to leave. But his plans are soon dashed when his car, bought and paid for, is gone. He tracks down the man responsible and in the process saves woman from the domed ring where she was to fight two zombies while people placed bets. This action lands Riley in jail.

Cholo gets together with his crew of marauders and they devise a plan to steal Dead Reckoning and then threaten to blow up Fiddler's Green unless they are paid. They make good on their plans but in the process of stealing the vehicle they allow a large group of Zombies through the first level of security to the city.

The Zombie army enters and quickly overwhelms the posted security teams. It soon becomes a feeding frenzy as the living are no match for the horde of zombies. They eat their way through and move on towards the main city, using their renewed skills to break through other defenses along the way.

Cholo contacts Kaufman and informs him of his plans to blow up Fiddlers' Green unless he gets paid. Reluctantly Kaufman makes a tentative agreement. He then contacts Riley and offers him a deal if he will stop Cholo. Riley having no alternative agrees. He is paired up with the girl from the ring and a couple of Kaufman's goons.

When Riley and his team are getting ready to leave they discover that the zombie's have entered the perimeter. Now the only way to survive both, the zombie attack or Cholo's attack is to stop Cholo and get Dead reckoning back.

For longer than most can remember water has been a natural barrier. It could protect the established settlements from competing marauders and zombies alike. Of course over the years there have been the occasional zombie to slip through but it was more by chance. Until now that is. The zombie horde follow their 'chosen' leader as he steps into the water, cross the river bed, and emerge on the other side. Free to roam and devour the living, who soon become trapped within the very defenses that once served to protect them.

Riley finally meets up with Cholo and with little incident manages to seize control of 'Dead Reckoning'. Cholo and his loyal followers are banished from the vehicle to fend for themselves. But Cholo gets bitten and slowly makes his way back towards Fiddlers' Green. Cholo makes his way into the parking garage just in time to catch Kaufman trying to escape…

Riley takes Dead Reckoning back to the city just in time to see the Zombie attacking the living. The living are trapped between the army of the dead and the electrified fence. Using the weapons of the truck they assist the survivors in their defense against the dead. Once the situation is contained Riley takes the opportunity to head north in hopes of finding a safer place.

Common Links:

Much of the story revolves around fuel (gas station attendant, fuel pumps)

Vast isolated places (void of the living)

Secured compounds

The on-going need for fuel

Armored vehicles

Wearing of leather and protective clothing

Shotguns and other firearms

Use of primitive weapons

A downed aicraft

Use of a loud speaker

Conversations about the state of the world

Use of fire and dogs

Desolate roads and car chases

Musicians with brass instruments

Travelling north or to a better place

One of the special team members has a pad on his shoulder

Cage fights

SECTION III

-Stories Linked-

Australia and The United States, 1968(ish)

Common Links… well linked

How the stories are intertwined

How the world might handle such an outbreak

The future… if there was one

Australia and the United States, 1968(ish)

First of all what was the world like in 1968? The world's population was just over 3.5 billion (half of 2010). We didn't have cable TV, internet, divorce wasn't socially acceptable, global warming wasn't an agenda, political correctness didn't exist…

The United States saw an unemployment rate of 3.3 percent. The population was just over 200 million. For many, life was simple. The hippie movement was sweeping the nation, as were the civil rights movements, anti-war protests, and the Space Race was still in full swing (let's not forget the Cold War). By the 70's, America saw the global recession, fuel shortages, and the end of the draft.

In 1968 Australia, their population was about half of today's at almost 12 million. During the 60's and 70's they were already on their way to greater ties with the United States, breaking from their British roots. They supported America's efforts in Vietnam and with the anti-communist movement resulting from the Cold-War. They also saw greater representation of the Aboriginal Australians and increased rights for women during their civil rights movement. Their film industry finally began to take hold. Australia saw many changes within its government, and their involvement on the international scene, especially Asia and the Pacific areas. Like the US, Australia ended conscription (drafting soldiers) and they were being hit with the global recession.

The sixties saw many changes in technology, society, and greater exposure to the world scene (National Geographic aired on TV in 1964). The world was changing and soon it would never be the same. Some of the big events of 1968 were:

Simon & Garfunkel reach #1, Rowan & Martin's Laugh-In debuted on NBC, Grenoble, France hosted the 1968 Winter Olympic Games, the Tet Offensive (a military campaign during the Vietnam War), Martin Luther King Jr. was assassinated, the Gateway Arch opens in St. Louis, Missouri, U.S. presidential candidate Robert F. Kennedy was assassinated, Dr. Christian Barnard performs the first successful heart transplant, Ringo Starr temporarily quits The Beatles…, France explodes its first hydrogen bomb (becoming the world's fifth nuclear power), The Soviet Zond 5 spaceship, the first to fly around the Moon and re-enter the Earth's atmosphere, NASA launches Apollo 7, the first manned Apollo mission, The Beatles release The White Album, and Apollo 8 launched, the first manned mission around the moon.

Common links… well linked…

Now at first one might think it a stretch to place these two seemingly separate concepts into one reality. They were not produced in the same manner, the locations are on completely different continents (North America and Australia), and the story lines follow seemingly different ideas. However, that is not actually the case, it all depends on how close you are willing to look at the clues and links.

In fact, the two stories are very much intertwined. The clues are blatantly obvious if one just takes a moment to see them. After reviewing the above outlines for the various films one should be able to see the pattern as it emerges. The commonalities should already have begun to form, even to the non-believer.

It is highly recommended that you sit and watch the films in the order prescribed and take a moment to jot down your own notes. A Max/ Zombiathon weekend with your friends would do the trick nicely. Everyone sits and looks for the clues. Because I am sure that the films are littered with so many more clues than those I found while conducting my 'research'.

But here is another look at the common links of the various films:

Night of the Living Dead

The use of desolate roads, lone vehicles, and chases involving the vehicle

Johnny wears driving gloves

The theme of finding a strong hold and debating to stay or run

The small music box

Radiation fallout, from a satellite, is the possible cause

Ben was at a small diner when he witnessed attacks.

Fuel is a major factor, complete with fuel trucks and gas pumps

Tom, dark haired, is a 'driver'

Zombies grab at their prey

They use fire as a weapon

Police officers are shown helping restore order

The posse uses revolvers and shotguns

They have helicopters

Use dogs to help fight of attackers

Dawn of the Dead

The police officers being key characters

Use of a helicopter

Ongoing need for fuel

Use of shotguns and revolvers

Use of mannequin

Use of view finder

Leather clad bikers/marauders

One of the police officers is an expert driver

Use of semi truck

Need to head north

Use of fire to cremate the remains

Use of primitive weapons

Use of air ducts

The use of the nuclear option was described

Mad Max

Takes place after an unexplained holocaust

Main characters are both police officers and marauders

The use of shotguns and revolvers

Fuel tanker truck

Mannequins (shooting it in the head)

Fire and dogs

References (the zombie mask, him standing like a zombie)

Leather clad bikers and officers

Traveling north

People live in protected areas

Experienced drivers, driving gloves

Desolate roads and car chases

Max's wife plays the saxophone

The Road Warrior

Narration and conversations about the state of the world

World holocaust explained (nuclear)

Use of fire and dogs

Primitive weapons

Shotgun and revolver

Need for fuel/Fuel tanker truck

Pilot

Leather clad people

Armored vehicles/police cars

Desolate roads and car chases

Max still has tattered driving gloves

Travelling north

(Deteriorating driving gloves)

Day of the Dead

Barren empty streets

Use of helicopter

The need for fuel

Use of revolvers and other guns

Fortified compound

Use of a loud speaker

Vehicles and motor home

Beyond Thunderdome

Vast isolated places

Secured compounds

The on-going need for fuel

Armored vehicles

Wearing of leather and protective clothing

Shotguns and other firearms

Use of primitive weapons

Use of pilot/aircraft

Use of a loud speaker

Use of viewfinder

Narration and conversations about the state of the world

World holocaust described (nuclear)

Use of fire and dogs

Desolate roads and car chases

Travelling north or to a better place

Land of the Dead

Much of the story revolves around fuel (gas station attendant, fuel pumps)

Vast isolated places (void of the living)

Secured compounds

The on-going need for fuel

Armored vehicles

Wearing of leather and protective clothing

Shotguns and other firearms

Use of primitive weapons

A downed aicraft

Use of a loud speaker

Conversations about the state of the world

Use of fire and dogs

Desolate roads and car chases

Musicians with brass instruments

Travelling north or to a better place

One of the special team members has a pad on his shoulder

Cage fights

As you can see the movies are littered with similarities, if you watch closely you will catch even more than what was listed… One of the key factors linking these stories is simple, the fact that the nuclear option was used. They deal with the human struggle during and following both personal and global tragedy.

The ongoing need for fuel is a big reoccurring theme. The truck was out and the pump was dangerously far from the house. As they tried to fly north had a constant need to refuel the helicopter. The bikers were observed siphoning fuel from the tanker. The marauders were fighting for a functioning refinery. Again there was helicopter needing fuel. It came to refining pig waste for fuel. Then finally there was the fuel at the Fiddler's Green.

Not to mention all the subtle hints in regards to fuel. Scenes with British Petroleum in the back ground, mentioning of tanker trucks, showing/ using pumps, even the 'lead' zombie was from a gas station.

Speaking of fuel, the next most common link would be the vehicles. As the films progressed the vehicles became more armored and more tailored to the environment. But they were still a major element. From normal cars in the first films to Max's interceptor, Aunty's motorized army, to finally Dead Reckoning, there was a steady progression.

Same could be said for air travel. Helicopters were used early on, then a gyrocopter, a single engine plane, and finally a downed airliner. A downed plane was also shown in the last film. But as maintenance, parts, and fuel became a major issue air travel became less possible.

The weapons of choice were very similar. Some of the main weapons used were either shotguns or revolvers. As the need dictated and/or the easy accessibility of bullets decreased, the use of more primitive weapons, particularly the bow/arrow became more common. Occasional use of fire as a weapon was a common theme as well, the cocktails and the flame-throwers.

Some of the clues were more subtle such as Johnny's driving gloves in the beginning, Max with his gloves. Other clues include the music boxes, the viewfinders, and the use of brass instruments. A lot of the main characters were police officers or security personnel and the uniforms were usually black. And the constant need to go north or at least an unspecified safe area. Don't forget the zombie mask and references to zombies.

Further examples lie with the continuing reference to or use of semi trucks, in particular fuel trucks, heating/cooling ducts, neither film fully explains what happened (the actual cause of the world collapse). Obviously the undead overwhelmed the living and obviously the 'nuclear option' was used. But, we see things from the more 'normal' person's perspective. Of course they are all stronger characters, especially as the story lines progress but, they would have to be (remember the rules of 'ZombieLand' (2009 .

We are shown how society once lived and thrived. But then steadily all was lost. There is the constant struggle between those wishing to move forward with life (maybe even clinging to the past) and those wishing to survive by any means. This theme is apparent in all the films from the desolate farm house to Fiddler's Green (this city greatly parallels Bartertown, with its high tower, seedy underground (complete with fuel).

Another reoccurring theme, either directly or indirectly, are the deals which are made and then broken. Showing just how people will do almost anything to get what they want, especially when it means staying alive.

An estimated timeline of when the films took place.

Keeping in mind that this reflects the possibility of their universe not being the same as ours and once society collapsed dating accuracy is lost.

| Night of the Living Dead | Dawn of the Dead | Mad Max | The Road Warrior | The Day of the Dead | Beyond Thunderdome | Land of the Dead |

| 1968 | Late 1970's | 1980's | 1990's | 2005(?) |

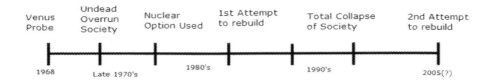

| Venus Probe | Undead Overrun Society | Nuclear Option Used | 1st Attempt to rebuild | Total Collapse of Society | 2nd Attempt to rebuild |

| 1968 | Late 1970's | 1980's | 1990's | 2005(?) |

How the two stories are intertwined

So far we have been given a synopsis of the films, a rundown covering many of the similarities, an introduction to personal conflicts which have shaped these realms, and even a small glimpse into the world before the apocalypse. But how might it have played out if the two were in fact connected, coexisting in the same realm of reality?

It may follow something like this:

Life is "normal". 1968, as mentioned, saw many changes. But no one could have been prepared for what was to come. The Venus probe (if that in fact was what triggered the events) was destroyed but, not before releasing a highly contagious and infectious disease. As the dust and debris slowly fall to Earth the winds blow the alien virus around the planet.

In a short time the virus germinates in the tissue of the recently deceased. However, it also can survive as an inactive virus in the living (everyone breaths it in). Once the virus runs its course the dead awaken with a vicious craving for living human flesh. Slowly at first, as it takes awhile for it fully spread. Authorities are not aware that there is even a problem, or refuse to acknowledge its existence. The attackers are viewed as 'crazies'. Judging by the times many would most like see them drug-crazed hippies and such.

It is not long though that everyone begins to realize this is more than mass anarchy organized by draft card burning dope-heads and reefer addicts or social outcast. But that the dead have actually risen up and returned as the walking living dead... undead.

Ben and the others had holed up in the farm house. Like them, millions around the word would have done the same. This would include a still innocent young Max Rockatansky and his family. From all walks of life, family, friends, neighbors and strangers alike would have banded together, not just out of loyalty or simple humanity, but out of the need to survive. Because at this time most would have thought this would pass. Even in a society as free as the United States was then, they still had faith that government was going to fix this.

It is quite possible that during this initial outbreak is when Max lost his father. He spoke about his father and his shiny shoes. How he regretted not telling his father how much he cared. This would have greatly affected Max, especially in the years to come…

After the initial outbreak, things did seem to be returning to normal. The National Guard, state and local law enforcement, and the federal government were getting a grip on things. The undead were fairly easy to capture and destroy (a blow to the head). Unfortunately, people continued to die (only to return…) and undead were roaming free not just locally but globally.

It takes a full decade for the army of the dead to outnumber the living. Still, the powers that be are slow to accept the realization that all is lost. They still hold on the hope that this crisis can be contained. The United Nations would have held conferences.

People had been living with this virus the same as a smallpox outbreak. Some would quarantine the undead, some would blatantly attack them and their living supporters, others would try to live and not get involved. Rights groups would try and protect the undead while others would see no coexistence.

Many people would have taken sides either way. The view of this would have varied with the area. The bible belt of the United States might have seen this as the rapture. The Middle East might view it as a plague upon the west. The Soviets would view it as a biological attack from the US, or at least tried to blame the United States (and perhaps visa versa). World leaders would bicker on what course of action needed to be taken.

Meanwhile, local authorities would deal with this in whatever manner seemed to be in the public's best interest (and perhaps get votes for the next election). As health organizations learned more about this, they would realize that a cure might not be possible. Military and law enforcement agencies would take matters in their own hands. Martial Law would have to be invoked, fostering more hatred of authority (especially in free societies like Australia and the United States). Military units would be placed in charge of enforcing curfews, collection/disposal of the dead, and enforcement of laws created in the spirit of public safety.

The virus had come on suddenly reanimating the dead at a slow but steady space. Initially the control of the outbreak would seem possible. But, after almost a decade the infected would spread more quickly and gain strength. Much like the proverbial snowball picking up momentum as it heads downhill.

Society would collapse like a demolished bridge and anarchy would reign. Everyone would fend for themselves as they flee the populated areas. Seeing this chaos mounting the governments would then look to the military for a final solution. The problem though, this solution would create an unforeseen paradox. To eliminate the undead, they must be willing to have acceptable losses (the killing of civilians still in the target zone). Well, the undead are already 'dead' so they were really only killing off those unlucky enough not evacuate. This adds to the numbers of the undead, thus the aforementioned paradox. Chemical warfare is ineffective, biological weapons wouldn't fare any better. Nukes destroy the area but resulting fallout/nuclear winter just adds to their numbers while in turn reducing ours.

The United Nations, an organization for world peace, would in fact be the cause of the world's demise. Or at least they greatly assisted its advancement. Nations would turn against nations, thus only creating more recruits to the army of the undead.

People would have no choice but abandon the major cities. Logic dictates that there is safety in numbers. There would be a need for protection from the undead as well as the marauders, bushrangers, and highwaymen roaming the countryside.

The idea of being able to live a normal life in a world gone mad would seem appealing. People would seek shelter and comfort wherever they could. Perhaps an isolated country home away from all people, maybe some large retail outlet (such as a shopping mall), while others would settle in small (hopefully) defendable communities.

Within these communities there would still be the desire for law and order, sense of normalcy. The police may at times not be much better than the social outcasts but, they were what was needed. Many would adapt to wearing leather as a form of protection from the bites of the undead.

Unfortunately history shows us how one group of people can't leave the other alone. The strong always try to take from the weak, the eternal struggle of good versus evil. We have lived through some form of crisis and everyone can handle only so much before reaching the breaking point.

The police deal with auto fatalities, and seeing them reanimate. It doesn't help if one must witness the death of a fellow police officer and friend, who then turns (Max's friend Goose). When the biker gang responsible hunts down Max's family it is the last straw. After seeking revenge, Max turns his back on this crumbling facsimile of society's rebirth.

Some people develop a survival strategy of going at it alone while others still hold on the social need for a community. But, there too is a fine line. Between those who wish to live and rebuild and those who wish to feed off the old world. People hold onto the dream of a place where everything is ok. In order to reach paradise, or to just exist one needs fuel. The bloodline of the world still holds a power over men.

Every day is fight to survive. The bushrangers/marauders are out to take everything they can. Even go so far as to tie the undead to their vehicles and parade them in from of their adversaries for the intimidation factor. Everyone has an angle of how to survive in this harsh new world. Deals and alliances are made... even if no one gains from the deals based on deceit.

Meanwhile, in bunkers at various strategic locations the governments had set up labs to study and hopefully find a cure. Shaky alliances were made between the military authority and the civilians. The search for survivors proves less and less likely, as does the hopes of finding a cure. The scientific mind is different than the military mind. While the military seeks a way to destroy this enemy, a scientist may seek a way to co-exist, perhaps even to domesticate them... Sometimes the fine line between sane and insane, good and bad is determined by the authority held instead of by the mental state of those in charge. Not everyone would fully appreciate such a pioneering approach.

As time passes the need for social interaction grows. Small villages sprout up where one can barter and trade for goods and services. In such a place, when someone has lost everything, one maybe able to get a fresh start, if they have skills. People are still people, they need bars and entertainment. Fighting has always been a thrill, from the gladiators of Rome to the WWF to the UFC/MMA, people love fights and cage matches.

But, to provide everything a city needs, they need fuel or perhaps methane to run its power generators. A resourceful little man could make it big in such a place, especially if he has a large and trained undead protector (though you may need to keep his head/mouth covered for safety).

When the world fell apart people took any means they could to escape. Some might be so desperate as to load up a plane full of babies and children. Leave the city behind and seek a safer place to hide. But the shockwave of a nuclear blast combined with the electromagnetic pulse (EMP) would be enough to bring down even large commercial jets. If the survivors were lucky enough they might find a mini paradise of their own. Even in such a paradise the zombie threat is still ever present, remember Co-Pilot who was jumped by Mr. Dead. As time goes by and babies grow into children, and children grow to be teens it would become apparent that they could not stay there forever and would have to see what was left of the old world.

They say what can one person do? Well depending on your point of view… He could either destroy everything or he could break a warlords grip, rescue a tribe of lost children, and rediscover what it means to be alive.

The world would go through many cycles as people fight to survive. Some might try to make it on their own, others would become primitive, while others would revert to a time of the feudal system. These would be hard times, lean times. At the same time, necessity is the mother of all inventions, technology may still progress in better equipped communities.

It would take a long time for people to build trust, or in some cases a dependency or others. Not every major city would have been destroyed. With some hard work and a lot of bullets a small army could clear out a city. It would be worth it, if that city was easy to defend, and offered plenty of protection from the elements. It would take a few years but, after about a decade or so it could be something nice. Under the right leadership the marauders could be organized, and serve the needs of the community.

Society would build, people would get comfortable and fall back into the old habits. There would again develop the caste system of haves and have nots. Treks would have to be made out of this protected city to gather needed supplies. The wealthy would rise to the top while using those under them. People would again find enjoyment in the little things. Sporting events, such as caged fights, would be a big draw, as would betting.

But even in such a place people would get greedy. They wouldn't be happy with the status quo. If leaders weren't careful they may build resentment and hatred within those that once served them. Then their protectors may in fact turn against them.

And what of the undead? If left unchecked, with few victims available, would they continue to thrive? Would suppressed memories or at least learned behavior resurface? Could the undead learn to live again, like their still breathing counterparts had done?

Only time would tell just how long it would take to develop a natural immunity to the virus. If one could wait long enough the dead would cease to exist. Though the rate of decay had been greatly reduced they wouldn't be able to last forever.

No one would know what the future would hold… Our world, that we knew, may become a thing of mythology.

How the world might handle such an outbreak

They say the weak shall inherit the Earth and only the strong will survive... in the case of a zombie holocaust both, in an odd sense, seem to be true!

Though the stories happen both during and after a major apocalyptic event, the story is shown mostly from the perspective of a small group of survivors. We are given glimpses of several radio broadcast, some news clips on the television and newspapers, and through narration, which shows this to be a worldwide epidemic. However, all the events are only seen through the experiences of small to medium sized groups of survivors.

If such a catastrophe were to have been real, it would have affected the entire world. In the beginning the attacks would have been isolated incidents. The occurrences of those attacks would steadily grow and the outbreak wouldn't take long to spread. Once it did it would have spread fast! The medical communities, governments would be caught by complete by surprise, without any real understanding or proper preliminary research studies conducted. By the time it was determined just how severe the threat was it would be too late. Society would have already collapsed and yet none of the world leaders would fully understand. Governments would go through the motions, same as with any other national crisis.

Emergency response teams would respond. Now this is very important. In 1968 (as stated above) there were limited means of mass communication. Limited federal support at the local level, The Federal Emergency Management Agency (FEMA) wasn't created until 1 April 1979, by Presidential Order. The concept of inter-agency cooperation was as much science fiction as was 'Star Trek' (1966-1969). Local Communities had to rely largely on their own resources. This was the same everywhere, in The United States, as well as, other 'developed' nations (West Germany, the United Kingdom, the USSR, and such) would have similar issues.

Now think about the less developed nations. They already had limited resources for dealing with day to day issues (famine, flood, and drought). Plus by 1968, the world had seen dozens of small wars, coups, uprisings, and riots. All which drained resources that could/should have been used elsewhere.

The World Health Organization (WHO) was formed in 1948 but, it too had seen its fair share of troubles. It suffered from budgetary problems, political infighting, and reduced resource contributions due to military spending. Its limited resources were largely in use in the Middle East, as the sixties saw many wars fought on its sands.

The major powers of the world were a non-trusting, secretive lot. They were so wrapped up in keeping the balance between the spread of communism and capitalism that they couldn't see the bigger picture of what was happening. The world was about to be crushed by a new and more destructive threat.

This is most likely the event that spawned nations like France to get onboard with the atom weapons development.

Recent history has proven just how quickly anarchy can rule after social order breaks down. It is actually surprising just how quickly a society can collapse once the governing powers are removed. Sure martial law may be imposed, economic/medical aid will arrive, and in time everything can return to normal. But in the meantime chaos will prevail.

One only needs to review resent events for the proof of just how quickly this can happen. Obvious examples are; Iraq in 2003 after the fall of Baghdad, New Orleans after Hurricane Katrina in 2005, and Haiti after the 2010 earthquake, each of which happened just within the first decade of the 21st century. Something else to keep in mind, these had working governments (Iraq not so much), the civil authorities were still present, the international communities were pouring in to assist, and they were localized, with only one being the result of military action.

With that in mind, remember the timeline of this event... it was 1968, when the initial outbreaks occurred. Which were then followed by about a ten year window, before all hope was lost and the epidemic had gotten out of control. Now if one were to follow those events it, at first glance, seems fairly clear as to what happened. However if one looks closer at the world in that time, the social systems in place, economic systems, and the political tensions the vision tends to get more and more clouded.

The Cold War was in full swing. The Soviet backed Warsaw Pact countries were deeply separated from the NATO Alliance. The United States and Russia were engaged in several 'competitions'. We had the 'Space Race', the 'Arms Race', Vietnam, and list goes on. The European Empires were steadily losing their hold on the various territories in Southeast Asia and Africa. The Middle East was gaining in power and influence, taking back control of their vast oil revenues and building stronger self-governed nations.

It was also a time before the internet, cable television, cell phones and all these luxuries that we take for granted today. The information super-highway was at times nothing more than small county road, which consisted of the nightly news, newspapers, word of mouth, or 'snail'-mail. It would take longer for one to become aware of issues in parts of their own area, much less the rest of the world. It can be argued that people may have also been less informed on the issues, due to the lack of readily available information. Furthermore the governments would be able to control the flow of information, to better control the population's reactions to such an epidemic. This last point would have been especially true in places like the Former USSR, Yugoslavia, China, the Middle East, parts of South America, and Africa.

If historic trends are any example of possible scenarios, disease and virus are more rampant in less developed areas, areas lacking in higher education, and impoverished/war torn regions. Historical examples would be The Black Death which is estimated to have killed 30% to 60% of Europe's population by 1400, the 1918 flu pandemic which resulted in 50 to 100 million people killed worldwide with an estimated 500 million infected by 1920, and HIV/AIDS has killed approximately 25 million and infected an additional 33 million worldwide since 1981. So if our world was hit with such a virus that had no known cure, no known antidote, and absolutely no means of prevention it is safe to assume it would overrun humankind in no time.

One of the theories proposed as to the cause of this virus, it was caused by the downed Venus satellite. That would give the analyst, doctors, and scientist a reasonable starting reference point to study the spread of the virus. With the assumption it entered the atmosphere over the Pacific the radiation would have spread across the US first before hitting Europe and Asia. It may have not been in full strength as it floated south into the Southern Hemisphere. Perhaps in places like Australia it was the newly deceased which were infected and not those already dead for an extended time. Or perhaps varying weather conditions would have an adverse effect on the virus, wetter climates promote growth while drier climates hinder the virus' development.

This again is based off of past events. During World War One gas was often used, it had a tendency to settle in lower areas, trenches and bomb craters. The first clues to the Chernobyl incident, outside the Soviet Union, were in Sweden approximately 700 miles away, and almost 36 hours after the meltdown. Another example was during the 1930's when the Midwest experienced severe droughts, the dust of the storms are said have blown as far east as New York, two days after the storm had occurred. Some accounts claim the dust travelled all the way to Europe in the following weeks.

In places where the government maintained tight controls over the population the reaction to the epidemic would have been vastly different than in the more open and freer societies. In such a case the stricter forms of government would have prevailed in containing the spread… at first. The United Nations would have held emergency sessions. NATO's reaction would not have been the same as it might be today, they might not have been so quick to consider Military intervention, especially on US soil.

However, it is highly likely that the Americas would have been put on a quarantine list to prevent possible spread, something like 'Outbreak' (1995) but on a much larger scale like '28 Weeks Later'(2007). In a futile effort to contain the spread, the world would have isolated some of greatest biologist and researchers of the time. Maybe they were not great due to actual talent but the larger budgets and resources at their disposal.

Quarantine is a very real possibility, such was the case during the smallpox outbreak in Yugoslavia in 1972. The WHO actually implemented an extensive quarantine, and the government instituted martial law in an effort to control and isolate the problem.

This would have been a valuable political tool during the Cold War. The Soviets more than likely would want to encourage such a bold restriction on their main stumbling block in their quest for world influence. This of course would have been foolish, being that this was in fact a worldwide issue. But such an outbreak, with a 'national' quarantine as a means of protection, might have been the very thing needed to allow the Soviet Union the opportunity to gain dominance in a paranoid and fearful Europe.

The Middle East might have been able to reduce the influence of the west, if this was seen as a sign of America's punishment for our lack morals. Some of the Dictators of various nations might have taken advantage of this, as their opportunity to advance their control and power. This would then cause a domino effect as the wars increased the population's death count, which eventually would increase the army of the undead.

Meanwhile, in places like Canada, Australia, and the United States the government would be slow to overly react, as not wanting to impede on the civil liberties and rights of its citizens. This would prevent early detection and isolation of the infected. They would be looking for a political solution as opposed to a military solution.

One of the great paradoxes of our world, an overly free society will eventually fall to ruin by being overly liberal and not maintaining proper controls in matters of public concern. While an overly aggressive and controlling government would eventually fall by oppressing their citizens. In a universe where the dead reanimate and rise to feed on the living, neither is the proper solution.

It would only be a matter of time before both sides came to the conclusion that there was one solution. The only obvious answer was the complete annihilation of the infected areas. The final solution as it were, or as some world say the 'Nuclear Option'.

Since the end of the Second World War the world had been preparing for the next big event. The leaders of our world had been planning, not only how to fight but how to survive World War III. Huge arsenals had been built and shelters were constructed. At that time even the everyday person already lived in fear of nuclear war. But no one was prepared for this.

The enemy was not those 'evil pinko commies' or 'those capitalist pigs' it was in fact the reanimated corpses of family and friends. Grandmothers, religious leaders, teachers, hippies, and soldiers no one was safe from the outbreak. The realization of this would have been devastating to the very core.

Leaders who were once enemies, those who had survived the horrors of global wars past were now called upon to find a solution. They sat in meetings, surrounded by armed security not to defend against each other... but for combined protection. They talked of the available options, to save the nations of the world, because this meant the very survival of the human race. So with heavy hearts it was decided.

The United States and the Soviet Union had the largest stock piles of Nuclear Arms, followed by the United Kingdom, France, China, and India. Though many would say Israel, South Africa, and Pakistan were equipped with nuclear arms. The US as a NATO member country would have armed Belgium, West Germany, Italy, the Netherlands, Turkey, and possibly Canada and Greece. At the same time, the Soviets would have armed various 'holdings' and allies with nuclear arms. This of course does not include ocean going vessels (ships and submarines), aircraft, and the possibility of space platforms.

Such a meeting would have started with heavy finger pointing as to who was to blame. The moral obligation to help the current survivors find shelter, the financial cost to clean up after, and what form of government would exist in the aftermath. After many heated debates and days of negotiations the orders were signed.

Somewhere around 1979 or 1980 the superpowers made their first strategic strikes. Missile silos everywhere opened and a loud roar was heard followed by a white line of smoke. Then some thousand or more miles away the major populated areas were hit.

The world leaders sat silently as they pelted their own communities, the outside world was now a total loss. But they could rest comfortable knowing they were safe in the shelters. Well that was until the first heart attack...

The future… if there was one

The 'why' it happened may be a little fuzzy but the 'what happened' is clearly defined. Now the only remaining questions are related to the future of the world and the future of the human race. Eventually it can be assumed the numbers of the dead would dwindle… as the bodies decompose, are eaten by wild/feral animals, or eliminated by human survivors.

It can further be safely assumed that if this virus was like any of the hundreds that have existed prior to this outbreak, it won't last. Either it will fade, weaken, or we will eventually build a natural immunity as healthy living people are born into this world. There would also be a strong likelihood of an actual vaccine being found. In other words, we would survive…

Of course, no one truly knows what the future holds. But if a worldwide epidemic of almost biblical proportions was to infect the world, what would the future hold? Could humanity realistically survive and rebuild. The short answer is yes. History holds the key to finding the answer.

Earlier it was mentioned the large number of people who had died from actual historically recorded past virus and/or disease related outbreaks. An equally yet depressing number have been killed in our vast and not too distant wars of the past century. World War One (WWI) had an estimated total of 37 million casualties and World War Two (WWII) had a staggering 60 million! Just the Battle of Stalingrad, basically the fight over one city, created almost two million casualties.

The Early part of the 20th century saw a large number of death causing conflicts (approximately 120 labeled as 'war' (see list in back). From disease to war it could easily be counted as a quarter or more of the world's population died. Yet somehow we have managed to grow to an unimaginable number of almost 7 billion people! In 1950 we were estimated to have only 1.5 billion people on the planet… think of how much we have grown in 60 or so years. That growth rate is with war, famine, disease, disasters, murder, natural deaths and accidents.

So it is safe to assume that mankind would survive an outbreak even of this magnitude. We might end up actually having a 'living' population that is less than what it was 10,000 years ago, an estimated 5 million worldwide, but we would have a good start (the Ark only had 8 people to rebuild with…)

It would also be safe to assume that eventually some team of scientist, if given enough time, resources, and test subjects would eventually find a cure, a vaccine, or a solution to combat the spread of the virus. Because we can't forget, there were many still hiding in bunkers and other 'safe havens'. Technology would continue to advance, maybe at less than impressive pace or maybe by leaps and bounds, but great advancements would be made. While in other less technologically savvy hideouts people may not be so inventive and might even slide backwards to a more primitive existence.

It can be hard to imagine, though it might be something like H.G. Wells 'Things to come' (1936). After years of protected isolation, those hiding out in the bunkers, finally return to reclaim the world from the marauders and zombies alike. Maybe we will end up like 'Logan's Run' (1976), where death is just another beginning and is actually worshiped… Perhaps the final outcome can be summed up by Josh Whedon's 'Serenity' (2005), and everyone finally abandons the "Earth that was" for a chance at a new life (that could help further explain the Reavers). The exact opposite could also be true, much like 'The Planet of the Apes' (1968), where we ceased being the top of the food chain, no longer the dominate species as it were. The last possibility would be 'BattleStar Galactica' (2004…), when they finally get to 'Earth' and it has been completely destroyed and void of human life…

So it really just depends on your view, if you are a 'glass half full' person or a 'glass half empty' person. I follow the 'Terminator' (1984) idea of "no fate but what we make". Our race has accomplished so much from so little that if Atlantis could be built thousands of years ago, who knows what is possible.   Perhaps much like the Greek mythology our world would become that of legend and fantasy.

Only the future knows for sure.

SECTION IV

-Misc Information-

Basic Trivia and Facts on the Films

Romero and Miller Basic Bios…

Film and Fan Based Websites

Basic Trivia and Facts on the Films

With so much being spent on analyzing the films, creating a conspiracy theory that they are related, and building a basic timeline it only seemed fitting to include some other information. So, what has been compiled, is a little basic trivia and facts on each film.

For each of the 7 films some basics, written by, directed by, genre, runtime, budget, distribution, and individual film trivia/facts for each. You can go to the Internet Movie Data Base (IMDB), Wikipedia, the movie homepages, and even fan based websites if you wish further information. There is so much information out there! I barely scratched the surface.

Of course following the spirit of this essay, the films are listed as the 'events' happened…

Night of the Living Dead

Written by: George A. Romero and John A. Russo

Directed by: George A. Romero

Genre: Horror, Sci-Fi, Thriller

Run time: 96 minutes

Budget: $114,000

Distributed by: The Walter Reade Organization

Basic Trivia/Facts:

The word 'zombie' is never used, instead other terms such as 'those things' are used.

This film was largely influenced by Herk Harvey's 'Carnival of Souls' (1962).

Both writers had a cameo George Romero (as a reporter) and John Russo (as a zombie).

The movie was filmed in Pennsylvania.

Tom Savini was originally hired to do the makeup effects for this film. However, He was unable to, do to being called to duty by the US Army to serve as a combat photographer in Vietnam.

Movie quote:

Newscaster: "It has been established that persons who have recently died have been returning to life and committing acts of murder. A widespread investigation of funeral homes, morgues, and hospitals has concluded that the unburied dead have been returning to life and seeking human victims. It's hard for us here to be reporting this to you, but it does seem to be a fact."

Dawn of the Dead

Written by: George A. Romero

Directed by: George A. Romero

Genre: Action, Horror, Science Fiction

Run time: 126 minutes

Budget: $650,000

Distributed by: United Film Distribution Company

Basic Trivia/Facts:

The term 'zombie' was actually used.

Many of the 'zombies' actors were actual amputees.

George Romero has a cameo, the director at the TV studio and as the Santa Claus biker.

It was filmed in Pennsylvania at the Monroeville Mall, during after hours.

Movie quote:

Dr. Foster: "This situation must be controlled before it's too late. They're multiplying too rapidly!"

Mad Max

Written by: George Miller and Byron Kennedy

Directed by: George Miller

Genre: Action, Adventure, Science Fiction

Run time: 93 minutes

Budget: $350,000

Distributed by: Village Roadshow Pictures

American International Pictures

Warner Brothers

Basic Trivia/Facts:

The film was inspired by 'A Boy and His Dog' (1975).

Only Mel Gibson's costume was actual leather, the other police officers were wearing vinyl costumes.

The only voice not dubbed for the American release was the Lounge Singer. Even Mel Gibson's voice was dubbed.

It was filmed in and around Melbourne, Australia.

Max's yellow interceptor car, a Ford Falcon XB sedan, was an actual a police car from the Australian state of Victoria, another yellow interceptor, a Ford Falcon XA GCI, was a decommissioned taxi cab.

Movie quote:

Max: "I'm scared, Fif. It's that rat circus out there, I'm beginning to enjoy it. Look, any longer out on that road and I'm one of them, a terminal psychotic, except that I've got this bronze badge that says that I'm one of the good guys."

The Road Warrior

Written by: George Miller and Terry Hayes

Directed by: George Miller

Genre: Action, Adventure, Science Fiction, Thriller

Run time: 95 minutes

Gross: $24,000,000

Distributed By: Warner Brothers

Basic Trivia/Facts:

At the time, it was the most expensive Australian film produced.

More than 80 vehicles were involved in the production.

After the first film was finished, all of the cars were supposed to be destroyed, including the black interceptor. But someone thought the interceptor should be saved from the crusher. During the preproduction for this film, someone found out about the interceptor, bought it back.

Max's car was a 1973 Ford Falcon XB GT Coupe, a car exclusive to Australia. A limited number of these cars were exported by Ford to New Zealand and the United Kingdom, but never to North America.

Max eats a can of "Dinki-Di" dog food, "Dinki-Di", Australian slang for "genuine" or "real."

Inspired by Akira Kurosawa's samurai films and Joseph Campbell's book "The Hero With a Thousand Faces."

Movie quote:

Pappagallo: "Do you think you're the only one that's suffered? We've all been through it in here. But we haven't given up. We're still human beings, with dignity. But you? You're out there with the garbage. You're NOTHING."

Day of the Dead

Written by: George A. Romero

Directed by: George A Romero

Genre: Action, Adventure, Horror, Science Fiction

Run time: 102 minutes

Budget: $3,500,000

Distributed by: United Film Distribution Company

Basic Trivia/Facts:

The book given to Bub is Stephen King's "Salem's Lot."

George Romero makes a cameo as a zombie.

Bud is the only Romero zombie to actually speak, "Hello Aunt Alicia." However, there is also a debatable scene where Bub may or may not have another line of dialogue. When Sarah enters Frankenstein's lab, she is startled when Bub emerges from the shadows behind her. After this, he moans something that many believe is, "I'm sorry."

Like the previous films, it was filmed in Pennsylvania however, there are several scenes done in Florida.

Movie quote:

Dr. Logan: "We don't have enough ammunition to shoot them all in the head. The time to have done that would have been in the beginning. No, we let them overrun us. We are in the minority now, something like 400,000 to one by my calculation."

Mad Max Beyond Thunderdome

Written by: Terry Hayes and George Miller

Directed by: George Miller and George Ogilvie

Genre: Action, Adventure, Science Fiction

Run time: 107 minutes

Budget: $12,000,000

Distributed by: Warner Brothers

Basic Trivia/Facts:

Max's character was actually an afterthought, the film was supposed to be about a group of children living without parents in the wild, who get found... it was decided that Max finds them.

Aunty Entity's (Tina Turner) steel mail dress weighed more than 55 kilograms (almost 120 pounds)!

 The outcomes on the Wheel are: - Death - Hard Labour - Acquittal - Gulag - Aunty's Choice - Spin Again - Forfeit Goods - Underworld - Amputation - Life Imprisonment.

Influences or references are from various sources, 'The Atomic Café' (1982), the restaurant's name. 'Fist Full of Dollars' (1964), Sergio Leone's western pitting the main character, a drifter (Clint Eastwood), playing the two opposing gangs against each other. Finally, 'Tommy' (1975), with the father-figure/savior/pilot, Captain Walker and Tina Turner who was the 'Acid Queen".

Movie quote:

Max: "I ain't Captain Walker. I'm the guy who carries Mr. Dead in his pocket."

Land of the Dead

Written by: George A. Romero

Directed by: George A. Romero

Genre: Action, Adventure, Horror, Science Fiction, Thriller

Run time: 97 minutes

Budget: $15,000,000

Distributed by: Universal Pictures

Basic Trivia/Facts:

The name of the high rise, "Fiddler's Green" is a song about the place where cavalrymen go when they die located "Halfway down the trail to hell".   It is also considered the final resting place for pirates.

George Romero has a cameo, but only his voice, during the puppet show, "Take that, you smelly zombie."

Was not filmed in Pennsylvania, as the others were, but in Toronto and then made to resemble Pittsburgh's geography.

Tom Savini, an actor, special effects, stuntman, was in and/or worked on three of the films, 'Dawn of the Dead' as a biker, 'Day of the Dead' as a make-up artist, and 'Land of the Dead' as a zombie. He was also in the remake 'Dawn of the Dead' (2004) as a county sheriff.

Movie quote:

Riley: "Isn't that what we're doing? Pretending to be alive?"

Romero and Miller Basic Bios...

Both Romero and Miller have had long careers. They have, and hopefully will continue to bless us with creative, imaginative, and entertaining tales. Both were born around the time of WWII, saw many historic events, the Korean War, the Berlin Airlift, the Cuban Missile Crisis, the birth of Rock-n-Roll, Vietnam, man on the moon, the collapse of the Soviet Union... and many more events that shaped the world we live in today.

Through their visions we get a glimpse into the mindset of so many. The fears of biological and/or nuclear holocaust were all to true. (The world almost saw WWIII on more than one occasion.) Whether the intent was to create such inspirational works of art, which are studied and viewed not only by the original fans but, continue to gain new ones... that is the outcome.

They helped shape and maybe even change to face of Hollywood because of their lasting impact on the film industry and society.

The following contains just the bare basic information. I am sure you can find even more information if you look up their fan based websites, or other such outlet.

George A. Romero Basic bio...

Born:

(George Andrew Romero)
February 4, 1940 (1940-02-04)
New York, NY, U.S.

Credits:

Film Producer, Film Director, Screenwriter, Editor, and Actor

Working in film:

(Most of his life...)

Filmography...

1968 Night of the Living Dead

1971 There's Always Vanilla

1973 The Crazies

1973 Season of the Witch

1978 Martin

1978 Dawn of the Dead

1981 Knightriders

1982 Creepshow

1985 Day of the Dead

1985 Document of the Dead

1987 Creepshow 2

1987 Drive-In Madness

1988 Monkey Shines

1990 Tales from the Darkside: The Movie

1990 Two Evil Eyes

1990 Night of the Living Dead

1991 The Silence of the Lambs

1993 The Dark Half

2000 Bruiser

2000 The American Nightmare

2004 Dawn of the Dead

2005 Land of the Dead

2005 Midnight Movies: From the Margin to the Mainstream

2008 Diary of the Dead

2008 Dead On: The Life and Cinema of George A. Romero

2009 Deadtime Stories

2009 Survival of the Dead

2010 The Crazies

2010 Deadtime Stories 2

2011 Into the Dark: Exploring the Horror Film

George Miller Basic bio...

Born:

(George Miliotis)
3 March 1945 (1945-03-03)
Brisbane, Queensland, Queensland, Australia

Credits:

Film Producer, Film Director, Screenwriter (and Physician)

Working:

1970 – Present

Filmography...

1979 Mad Max

1981 Mad Max 2: The Road Warrior

1983 Nightmare at 20,000 Feet

1983 The Dismissal

1985 Mad Max Beyond Thunderdome

1987 The Witches of Eastwick

1987 The Year My Voice Broke

1989 Dead Calm

1991 Flirting

1992 Lorenzo's Oil

1995 Babe

1998 Babe: Pig in the City

2006 Happy Feet

2011 Happy Feet 2

2012 Mad Max: Fury Road

2012 The Odyssey

Film/Fan Based Websites

There seems to be countless websites out there about these films and the great filmmakers who blessed us with these gems. I listed only a couple of sites from there you can find links to further your desire to learn more about these extraordinary filmmakers and the films that continue to influence the way certain genres are presented...

www.georgearomero.com
(Official site...)

www.homepageofthedead.com
(Fan based site)

www.madmaxmovies.com
(Info about the films...)

www.madmaxcars.com
(Title says it all...)

www.imdb.com
(Internet Movie Database)

www.zombiehunters.org/
(The name says it all)

www.kingzombie.com/
(Zombie related merchandise)

www.rottentomatoes.com
(Movie reviews)

SECTION V

-The People who Died-

Last Breath

Though this section is related to various death rates, it is perhaps best to start with birth rates and basic population stats. The world population has been steadily growing since the end of the 'Black Death' around 1400. Since then birth rates have continued to outnumber death rates, at least for now... at the current rate the population is expected to reach 9 billion by 2040. Currently (2010) the world population is estimated at just fewer than 7 billion. World births seem to have leveled off at 134 million per year since the 1990s, while the death rate is approximately 58 million per year.

The following lists can be broken into four different samplings of just how many people die... or should it be said, have died in the past years.

Since the zombie outbreak can be attributed to some sort of virus or disease the first list is for major plagues throughout history. Here are listed only some of the best documented cases.

The next is a list of what is officially classified as 'War' and the death toll attributed to that. The following is a list of death as a result of some natural disaster (tornado, hurricane...). Both lists are taken from the 20th century, approximately 100 years of war and disaster, with only key/large scale events mentioned.

The next group is a breakdown of the causes of death in the Unites States. After doing some researching it was decided to use two different dates, using collected data for 2002 and 2006.

The final grouping is for causes of death worldwide, broken down by what is classified as 'developed' and 'developing' nations. These are for the years of 2002 and 2004.

Though an extensive search was made to find the data listed (and much information was found), it was decided to choose just a random sample. The lists are for what is considered official wars, disasters, and other such causes. They do not include guerilla activity, minor conflicts, drug /gang related 'wars' and smaller natural events. The lists are only accurate with the information received and reported. None of the totals should be considered 100% accurate, the actual numbers could be more or less, and does not include those who died at a later date but as a direct result of participation in a war or particle event.

This information was collected (both what was used here and for other previous chapters) from various sources, government websites, The CDC (Center for Disease Control), the WHO (the World Health Organization), even Wikipedia, and several other sources. Though these may not be full lists, they do give a good idea as to just how many people have perished in the past, during major events.

Knowing this information, one could help prepare for the ultimate what if… the dead did rise!

One last bit of information:

An epidemic is defined as an outbreak of a contractible disease, which then spreads quickly through the population. A pandemic is then defined as an epidemic that is of a global nature. Something like the swine flu was an epidemic as it spread through Mexico and then became a pandemic when it crossed overseas causing alarm globally…

Major plague outbreaks

(Well-documented outbreaks of plagues or disease,
location, year, and agent type.)

European plague (1400 BC)
agent: unknown
Great Plague of Athens (430–427 BC)
agent: bubonic plague/smallpox/measles/typhus/anthrax/typhoid?
Antonine Plague (165–180)
agent: smallpox/measles?
Plague of Cyprian (250)
agent: smallpox/measles?
Plague of Justinian (541–542)
agent: bubonic plague or possibly viral hemorrhagic plague
Plague of Emmaus (18 A.H. / 639 A.D.)
agent: unknown
Plague of Constantinople (747–748)
The "Black Death" of 1347–1351
Great Plague of England (1348–1350)
agent: hemorrhagic plague
Great Plague of Ireland (1348–1351)
agent: hemorrhagic plague
Great Plague of Scotland (1348–1350)
agent: hemorrhagic plague
Great Plague of Portugal, the so called Peste Negra (1348–1348)
agent: hemorrhagic plague
Great Plague of Russia (1349–1353)

agent: hemorrhagic plague
Great Plague of Iceland (1402–1404)[1]
agent: hemorrhagic plague
American Epidemics (Results of Columbian Exchange) (1492-1950s?)
agent: cholera, influenza, malaria, measles, scarlet fever, smallpox, tuberculosis, typhoid, yellow fever
Plague of 1575, Italy, Sicily and segments of Northern Europe (1571–1576)
agent: hemorrhagic plague
London Plague (1592–1594)
agent: hemorrhagic plague
Italian Plague of 1629–1631 or Great Plague of Milan (1629–1631)
agent: hemorrhagic plague
Plague causing the end of the Ming Dynasty in China (1641-1644)
agent: unknown
Great Plague of Seville (1649)
agent: hemorrhagic plague
Great Plague of London (1665–1666)
agent: hemorrhagic plague
Great Plague of Vienna (1679–1670s)
agent: hemorrhagic plague
Great Plague of Marseille (1720–1722)
agent: possibly bubonic plague?
Russian plague of 1770-1772
agent: possibly bubonic plague?
The Third Pandemic, originated in China (1855–1950s)
agent: bubonic plague.
1994 plague epidemic in Surat
agent: possibly pneumonic plague?

20th Century's Official 'Wars'

(Year-Nations involved-Death Toll)

1886-1908: Belgium-Congo Free State (8 million)
1899-02: British-Boer war (100,000)
1899-03: Colombian civil war (120,000)
1899-02: Philippines vs USA (20,000)
1900-01: Boxer rebels against Russia, Britain, France, Japan, USA against rebels (35,000)
1903: Ottomans vs Macedonian rebels (20,000)
1904: Germany vs Namibia (65,000)
1904-05: Japan vs Russia (150,000)
1910-20: Mexican revolution (250,000)
1911: Chinese Revolution (2.4 million)
1911-12: Italian-Ottoman war (20,000)
1912-13: Balkan wars (150,000)
1915: the Ottoman empire slaughters Armenians (1.2 million)
1915-20: the Ottoman empire slaughters 500,000 Assyrians
1916-23: the Ottoman empire slaughters 350,000 Greek Pontians and 480,000 Anatolian Greeks
1914-18: World War I (20 million)
1916: Kyrgyz revolt against Russia (120,000)
1917-21: Soviet revolution (5 million)
1917-19: Greece vs Turkey (45,000)
1919-21: Poland vs Soviet Union (27,000)
1928-37: Chinese civil war (2 million)
1931: Japanese Manchurian War (1.1 million)
1932-33: Soviet Union vs Ukraine (10 million)

1934: Mao's Long March (170,000)
1936: Italy's invasion of Ethiopia (200,000)
1936-37: Stalin's purges (13 million)
1936-39: Spanish civil war (600,000)
1937-45: Japanese invasion of China (500,000)
1939-45: World War II (55 million) including holocaust and Chinese revolution
1946-49: Chinese civil war (1.2 million)
1946-49: Greek civil war (50,000)
1946-54: France-Vietnam war (600,000)
1947: Partition of India and Pakistan (1 million)
1947: Taiwan's uprising against the Kuomintang (30,000)
1948-1958: Colombian civil war (250,000)
1948-1973: Arab-Israeli wars (70,000)
1949-: Indian Muslims vs Hindus (20,000)
1949-50: Mainland China vs Tibet (1,200,000)
1950-53: Korean war (3 million)
1952-59: Kenya's Mau Mau insurrection (20,000)
1954-62: French-Algerian war (368,000)
1958-61: Mao's "Great Leap Forward" (38 million)
1960-90: South Africa vs Africa National Congress (?)
1960-96: Guatemala's civil war (200,000)
1961-98: Indonesia vs West Papua/Iran (100,000)
1961-2003: Kurds vs Iraq (180,000)
1962-75: Mozambique Frelimo vs Portugal (?)
1964-73: USA-Vietnam war (3 million)
1965: second India-Pakistan war over Kashmir
1965-66: Indonesian civil war (250,000)
1966-69: Mao's "Cultural Revolution" (11 million)
1966-: Colombia's civil war (31,000)
1967-70: Nigeria-Biafra civil war (800,000)
1968-80: Rhodesia's civil war (?)
1969-: Philippines vs New People's Army (40,000)
1969-79: Idi Amin, Uganda (300,000)
1969-02: IRA - Northern Ireland's civil war (2,000)
1969-79: Francisco Macias Nguema, Equatorial Guinea (50,000)
1971: Pakistan-Bangladesh civil war (500,000)
1972-: Philippines vs Muslim separatists (Moro Islamic Liberation Front, etc) (120,000)

1972: Burundi's civil war (300,000)
1972-79: Rhodesia/Zimbabwe's civil war (30,000)
1974-91: Ethiopian civil war (1,000,000)
1975-78: Menghitsu, Ethiopia (1.5 million)
1975-79: Khmer Rouge, Cambodia (1.7 million)
1975-89: Boat people, Vietnam (250,000)
1975-90: civil war in Lebanon (40,000)
1975-87: Laos' civil war (184,000)
1975-2002: Angolan civil war (500,000)
1976-83: Argentina's military regime (20,000)
1976-93: Mozambique's civil war (900,000)
1976-98: Indonesia-East Timor civil war (600,000)
1976-2005: Indonesia-Aceh (GAM) civil war (12,000)
1977-92: El Salvador's civil war (75,000)
1979: Vietnam-China war (30,000)
1979-88: the Soviet Union invades Afghanistan (1.3 million)
1980-88: Iraq-Iran war (1 million)
1980-92: Sendero Luminoso - Peru's civil war (69,000)
1980-99: Kurds vs Turkey (35,000)
1981-90: Nicaragua vs Contras (60,000)
1982-90: Hissene Habre, Chad (40,000)
1983-: Sri Lanka's civil war (70,000)
1983-2002: Sudanese civil war (2 million)
1986-: Indian Kashmir's civil war (60,000)
1987-: Palestinian Intifada (4,500)
1988-2001: Afghanistan civil war (400,000)
1988-2004: Somalia's civil war (550,000)
1989-: Liberian civil war (220,000)
1989-: Uganda vs Lord's Resistance Army (30,000)
1991: Gulf War - large coalition against Iraq to liberate Kuwait (85,000)
1991-97: Congo's civil war (800,000)
1991-2000: Sierra Leone's civil war (200,000)
1991-2009: Russia-Chechnya civil war (200,000)
1991-94: Armenia-Azerbaijan war (35,000)
1992-96: Tajikstan's civil war (50,000)
1992-96: Yugoslavian wars (260,000)
1992-99: Algerian civil war (150,000)
1993-97: Congo Brazzaville's civil war (100,000)
1993-2005: Burundi's civil war (200,000)

1994: Rwanda's civil war (900,000)
1995-: Pakistani Sunnis vs Shiites (1,300)
1995-: Maoist rebellion in Nepal (12,000)
1998-: Congo/Zaire's war - Rwanda and Uganda vs Zimbabwe, Angola and Namibia (3.8 million)
1998-2000: Ethiopia-Eritrea war (75,000)
1999: Kosovo's liberation war - NATO vs Serbia (2,000)
2001-: Afghanistan's liberation war - USA & UK vs Taliban (40,000)
2002-: Cote d'Ivoire's civil war (1,000)
2003: Second Iraq-USA war - USA, UK and Australia vs Saddam Hussein (14,000)
2003-09: Sudan vs JEM/Darfur (300,000)
2003-: Iraq's civil war (60,000)
2004-: Sudan vs SPLM & Eritrea (?)
2004-: Yemen vs Shiite Muslims (?)
2004-: Thailand vs Muslim separatists (3,700)

Arab-Israeli Wars

I (1947-49): 6,373 Israeli and 15,000 Arabs die

II (1956): 231 Israeli and 3,000 Egyptians die

III (1967): 776 Israeli and 20,000 Arabs die

IV (1973): 2,688 Israeli and 18,000 Arabs die

Intifada I (1987-92): 170 Israelis and 1,000 Palestinians

Intifada II (2000-03): 700 Israelis and 2,000 Palestinians

Israel-Hamas war (2008): 1,300 Palestinians

20ᵗʰ Century's 100 Deadliest Natural Disasters

Country	Year	Disaster	Region	Continent	Killed
Worldwide	1917	Epidemic	NA	ALL	20,000,000
Soviet Union	1932	Famine	Russia.Fed	Europe	5,000,000
China, P Rep	1931	Flood	E.Asia	Asia	3,700,000
China, P Rep	1928	Drought	E.Asia	Asia	3,000,000
NA	1914	Epidemic	Rest.Europ	Europe	3,000,000
Soviet Union	1917	Epidemic	Russia.Fed	Europe	2,500,000
China, P Rep	1959	Flood	E.Asia	Asia	2,000,000
India	1920	Epidemic	S.Asia	Asia	2,000,000
Bangladesh	1943	Famine	S.Asia	Asia	1,900,000
China, P Rep	1909	Epidemic	E.Asia	Asia	1,500,000
India	1942	Drought	S.Asia	Asia	1,500,000
India	1907	Epidemic	S.Asia	Asia	1,300,000
India	1900	Drought	S.Asia	Asia	1,250,000
NA	1957	Epidemic	NA	ALL	1,250,000
Soviet Union	1921	Drought	Russia.Fed	Europe	1,200,000
NA	1968	Epidemic	NA	ALL	700,000
Ethiopia	1972	Famine	E.Africa	Africa	600,000
China, P Rep	1920	Drought	E.Asia	Asia	500,000
China, P Rep	1938	Flood	E.Asia	Asia	500,000
China, P Rep	1939	Flood	E.Asia	Asia	500,000
India	1920	Epidemic	S.Asia	Asia	500,000
India	1965	Drought	S.Asia	Asia	500,000

India	1966	Drought	S.Asia	Asia	500,000
India	1967	Drought	S.Asia	Asia	500,000
India	1926	Epidemic	S.Asia	Asia	423,000
Bangladesh	1918	Epidemic	S.Asia	Asia	393,000
Bangladesh	1970	Cycl.Hurr. Typh	S.Asia	Asia	300,000
Ethiopia	1984	Drought	E.Africa	Africa	300,000
India	1924	Epidemic	S.Asia	Asia	300,000
China, P Rep	1976	Earthquake	E.Asia	Asia	242,000
China, P Rep	1927	Earthquake	E.Asia	Asia	200,000
Ethiopia	1974	Drought	E.Africa	Africa	200,000
Uganda	1901	Epidemic	E.Africa	Africa	200,000
China, P Rep	1920	Earthquake	E.Asia	Asia	180,000
Sudan	1984	Drought	N.Africa	Africa	150,000
Japan	1923	Earthquake	E.Asia	Asia	143,000
China, P Rep	1935	Flood	E.Asia	Asia	142,000
Bangladesh	1991	Cycl.Hurr. Typh	S.Asia	Asia	138,866
Soviet Union	1948	Earthquake	Russia.Fed	Europe	110,000
China, P Rep	1908	Flood	E.Asia	Asia	100,000
China, P Rep	1911	Flood	E.Asia	Asia	100,000
China, P Rep	1922	Cycl.Hurr. Typh	E.Asia	Asia	100,000
Ethiopia	1973	Drought	E.Africa	Africa	100,000
Mozambique	1985	Drought	E.Africa	Africa	100,000
Niger	1923	Epidemic	W.Africa	Africa	100,000
Italy	1908	Earthquake	Euro.Union	Europe	75,000
China, P Rep	1932	Earthquake	E.Asia	Asia	70,000
Peru	1970	Earthquake	S.America	Americas	66,794
NA	1972	Drought	W.Africa	Africa	62,500
NA	1973	Drought	W.Africa	Africa	62,500
NA	1974	Drought	W.Africa	Africa	62,500
Bangladesh	1942	Cycl.Hurr. Typh	S.Asia	Asia	61,000
China, P Rep	1910	Epidemic	E.Asia	Asia	60,000
India	1935	Cycl.Hurr. Typh	S.Asia	Asia	60,000

Pakistan	1935	Earthquake	S.Asia	Asia	60,000
China, P Rep	1949	Flood	E.Asia	Asia	57,000
India	1935	Earthquake	S.Asia	Asia	56,000
Canada	1918	Epidemic	N.America	Americas	50,000
China, P Rep	1912	Cycl.Hurr. Typh	E.Asia	Asia	50,000
Guatemala	1949	Flood	C.America	Americas	40,000
India	1942	Cycl.Hurr. Typh	S.Asia	Asia	40,000
Martinique	1902	Volcano	Caribbean	Americas	40,000
Bangladesh	1965	Cycl.Hurr. Typh	S.Asia	Asia	36,000
Iran, Islam Rep	1990	Earthquake	S.Asia	Asia	36,000
NA	1943	Drought	E.Africa	Africa	35,000
Turkey	1939	Earthquake	W.Asia	Asia	32,962
Cape Verde Is	1946	Drought	W.Africa	Africa	30,000
Chile	1939	Earthquake	S.America	Americas	30,000
China, P Rep	1954	Flood	E.Asia	Asia	30,000
Italy	1915	Earthquake	Euro.Union	Europe	30,000
Bangladesh	1974	Flood	S.Asia	Asia	28,700
Niger	1931	Famine	W.Africa	Africa	26,000
Soviet Union	1988	Earthquake	Russia.Fed	Europe	25,000
Cape Verde Is	1920	Drought	W.Africa	Africa	24,000
Guatemala	1976	Earthquake	C.America	Americas	23,000
Iran, Islam Rep	1939	Earthquake	S.Asia	Asia	23,000
Colombia	1985	Volcano	S.America	Americas	21,800
Niger	1910	Drought	W.Africa	Africa	21,250
Niger	1911	Drought	W.Africa	Africa	21,250
Niger	1912	Drought	W.Africa	Africa	21,250
Niger	1913	Drought	W.Africa	Africa	21,250
China, P Rep	1974	Earthquake	E.Asia	Asia	20,000
India	1905	Earthquake	S.Asia	Asia	20,000
Iran, Islam Rep	1978	Earthquake	S.Asia	Asia	20,000
Somalia	1974	Drought	E.Africa	Africa	19,000

China, P Rep	1933	Flood	E.Asia	Asia	18,000
China, P Rep	1930	Storm	E.Asia	Asia	15,000
Indonesia	1917	Earthquake	SE.Asia	Asia	15,000
India	1977	Cycl.Hurr. Typh	S.Asia	Asia	14,204
Bangladesh	1965	Cycl.Hurr. Typh	S.Asia	Asia	12,047
China, P Rep	1907	Earthquake	E.Asia	Asia	12,000
Iran, Islam Rep	1962	Earthquake	S.Asia	Asia	12,000
Morocco	1960	Earthquake	N.Africa	Africa	12,000
Soviet Union	1907	Earthquake	Russia.Fed	Europe	12,000
Soviet Union	1949	Landslide	Russia.Fed	Europe	12,000
Bangladesh	1963	Cycl.Hurr. Typh	S.Asia	Asia	11,500
Bangladesh	1961	Cycl.Hurr. Typh	S.Asia	Asia	11,000
Cape Verde Is	1900	Drought	W.Africa	Africa	11,000
Hong Kong (China)	1937	Cycl.Hurr. Typh	E.Asia	Asia	11,000
Nigeria	1991	Epidemic	W.Africa	Africa	10,391

Leading Causes of Death in the United States 2002

Cause of death - Number of Deaths
Major Cardiovascular Diseases: 936,923
Malignant Neoplasms: 553,091
Chronic Lower Respiratory: 122,009
Diabetes Mellitus: 69,301
Influenza and Pneumonia: 65,313
Alzheimers: 49,558
Motor Vehicle Accidents: 43,354
Renal Failure: 36,471
Septicemia: 31,224
Firearms: 28,663
Total (2,403,351)

Accidental Death – Number of Deaths

Motor Vehicle: 43,354
Unspecified non-transport: 17,437
Falls: 13,322
Poisonous Substances: 12,757
Drowning: 3,842
Exposure to Smoke, Fire, Flames: 3,377
Other Land Transport Accidents: 1,492
Complications of Medical Care: 3,059
Accidental Discharge of Firearms: 776
Total Number of Accidental (97,900)

Leading Causes of Death in the United States 2006

Heart disease: 631,636
Cancer: 559,888
Stroke (cerebrovascular diseases): 137,119
Chronic lower respiratory diseases: 124,583
Accidents (unintentional injuries): 121,599
Diabetes: 72,449
Alzheimer's disease: 72,432
Influenza and Pneumonia: 56,326
Nephritis, nephrotic syndrome, and nephrosis: 45,344
Septicemia: 34,234

In 'Developing' Countries- Total Number of Deaths (2002)

HIV-AIDS: 2,678,000
Lower respiratory infections: 2,643,000
Ischaemic heart disease: 2,484,000
Diarrhea: 1,793,000
Cerebrovascular disease: 1,381,000
Childhood diseases: 1,217,000
Malaria: 1,103,000
Tuberculosis: 1,021,000
Chronic obstructive pulmonary disease: 748,000
Measles: 674,000

In 'Developed' Countries - Total Number of Deaths (2002)

Ischaemic heart disease: 3,512,000
Cerebrovascular disease: 3,346,000
Chronic obstructive pulmonary disease: 1,829,000
Lower respiratory infections: 1,180,000
Lung cancer: 938,000
Car accident: 669,000
Stomach cancer: 657,000
Hypertensive heart disease: 635,000
Suicide: 499,000

Worldwide Leading Causes of Death 2004

(In millions)
Coronary heart disease: 7.20
Stroke and other cerebrovascular diseases: 5.71
Lower respiratory infections: 4.18
Chronic obstructive pulmonary disease: 3.02
Diarrhoeal diseases: 2.16
HIV/AIDS: 2.04
Tuberculosis: 1.46
Trachea, bronchus, lung cancers: 1.32
Road traffic accidents: 1.27
Prematurity and low birth weight: 1.18

Disclaimer:

To my knowledge George Miller and George A Romero never collaborated nor intentionally intended for a connection to be drawn between their films. This connection was of my own invention after viewing their films. Any connection is purely coincidental, to the best of my knowledge. The connections were drawn from my imagination as a true fan, with a deep appreciation for the films and those responsible for their creation.

Thank you Mr. Miller

Thank you Mr. Romero

Thank you to all the others who participated in their creation and production.